T0077955

PORTUGAL AND SPAIN ON THE "INTERNATIONAL ADVENTURER"

A FICTIONAL – HISTORICAL NARRATIVE

Mark J. Curran

www.trafford.com
North America & international
toll-free: 844-688-6899 (USA & Canada)
fax: 812 355 4082

DEDICATION

To the Professors Who Prepared Me for Portugal and Spain
and the Lindblad Expedition – National Geographic Explorer Friends
Who Inspired Me

CONTENTS

PART II - SPAIN

PROLOGUE

I'm flying to Madeira to rejoin the ship, crew, staff and adventurers for Adventure Travel's trip to this part of the world. AT's specialty, home based in Lisbon, is the Peninsula, Portugal's former possessions, mainly its old colony Brazil, and around the tip of Africa to India, Macau and finally Japan. This is my first chance at the "metrópoles" of Portugal and Spain and I'm excited. It is early June, 1977, still springtime and anticipated great weather for the expedition.

If you have read my books including the latest "Pre - Columbian Mexico – Plans, Pitfalls and Perils" you know what led to this trip. I'm Mike Gaherty a now Associate Professor of Spanish and Portuguese at the University of Nebraska in Lincoln. Research specialty has always been Brazil, but with the Spanish connection, great interest especially in Mexico, Guatemala, Copán in Honduras and the Pre – Columbian Civilization as well as the folk – popular poetry and woodcuts of the "corridos." But Ph.D. study started with the "mother" countries, Spain and Portugal. Books and academic articles on all the above brought the latest promotion ("dry" as they say due to a lack of funding in the economic downturn but the "raise" promised for some time soon; I may add, "if the crick don't rise"), now to the middle rank of Associate Professor. Okay.

I have a serious relationship with Amy Carrier, the Assistant Adventure Leader [AAL] on the "Adventurer." We met in 1973 on AT's trip to Brazil when I was hired on as "cultural speaker," got along well, and deepened the relationship in Mexico in Spring 1974 doing research for the 1975 AT trip to Mexico. When you have risked your lives and come close to death together it does strengthen bonds. I even bought an engagement ring after the 1974 research trip and planned on proposing to Amy that winter, but she said she "wasn't ready," a surprise to me. She said she wanted to wait after the return trip to Mexico in 1975, then back to Brazil in 1976, and now the trip to Portugal and Spain. I'm not sure why. We had really grown to know each other in all ways and thought we were meant for each other. But she promised that we could pursue all that "later." Hmm. She said she would put the ring somewhere for safekeeping. I was hurting a lot more on the inside than I showed on the outside. Maybe because this was not my first rodeo being bucked off right out of the chute.

In the past there had been old flames in Brazil but even before that an engagement to college girlfriend Molly in Washington D.C. Our wedding date had actually been set, arrangements in process when the whole thing blew up when Molly learned of my "amorous adventures" in Brazil. It seems so long ago. We are in touch, both still available but lots of water under that bridge. I call Molly every few months or so, we talk of past and present, but there is no movement along that line. So life goes on, I'm on the way to Madeira and then a new experience, my first time in Portugal or Spain in spite of earning a Ph.D. studying both countries (as well as Brazil and Mexico) in depth. There, you have it. Oh, I'm a "cradle Catholic," now a much evolved "progressive Catholic," and all these amorous ties were done in good faith. I don't know why I decided to mention that.

1

ARRIVAL IN MADEIRA, MIKE GOES ON BOARD THE "ADVENTURER"

I arrived at the airport in Madeira after the overnight flight from Boston, a harrowing experience in itself. The "landing strip" is a concrete runway about the width of a four -lane freeway in the U.S., built on and supported by a few dozen concrete columns on the edge of a steep hill by the sea. Just as well I did not know about that ahead of time. Once we landed, wings rocking in the wind, and almost coming up against the orange barriers at the end of the runway and then taxiing back to the terminal on "terra firme," all breathed a sigh of relief. I overheard one of the stewardesses say that pilots consider this the most dangerous place to land and take off in the world! Oh. Okay.

Suffering from jet lag, groggy from the overnight flight, I took a taxi (my first ride in a Mercedes, let alone a Mercedes taxi; Mike you're not in Brazil anymore with the VW Bug taxis) to the docks where "Adventurer" (and Amy) were waiting. The ship had come in from the end of its trip to Ireland, England and the Azores and most passengers were disembarking and heading home.

An aside. A surprise in the Madeira international airport, and different from white - dominated "official" Brazil, were all the crews of Angola,

1

Mozambique and even TAP [Transportes Aêreos Portugueses] airlines, crews who were black! You did not see this in Brazil. The airport was not a small operation when you add all the European airlines with that huge tourist business to Madeira. The spoken continental Portuguese threw me for a loop at first, missing most of it; that would change as we did our excursions in Portugal, using my favorite Portuguese phrase: "Fale mais devagar, sou do Brasil!" ["Speak more slowly; I'm from Brazil."]

The docks in Madeira with all the ocean liners and tourist ships from Europe were a bit overwhelming, but there was the sleek, white "Adventurer" I remembered from just last year's return trip to Brazil. The taxi arrived to the port entry and after a long wait with the usual bureaucracy (Portugal's main export to Brazil and vice - versa) I was ushered through the gate and lugged my pack and large bag to the gangway of the ship.

I was greeted by old friend Executive Officer Martim Mendes, this time given a big Portuguese "abraço," "Bemvindo Professor Miguel, estamos todos muito felizes te-lo a bordo de novo!" He ushered me aboard and escorted me to my old cabin in the passenger section, smiling, saying Susan Gillian of AT Personnel in Los Angeles had once again requested "comfortable lodging" for the American cultural guy. There would be the usual staff meeting and luncheon in the chart room at noon, a big reunion for most. He suggested a nap and shower to recover from the jet lag and left me to it. I had scarcely put the bags on the bed when the room telephone rang. "Oi meu amigo. I am so happy you are here. I'll come up right away and we can say hello."

"Great, Amy. I'm glad you are still talking to me."

Ten minutes later there was a knock on the door and there she was, beautiful as ever. She did not hesitate but came up, gave me a long kiss and hug and moved that luscious body close to mine. All returned with enthusiasm. The room was small so I sat on the one easy chair and she at the chair at the desk. (The bed was full of my unpacked luggage, at least for now; I thought it could be a good fit for companionship later.) She said she just had fifteen minutes or so, back to the staff desk getting ready for Lisbon two days from now.

"Mike, I guess you need an apology. Or at least an explanation. I have thought long and hard about my decision of too long ago, and cannot tell you how torn I was and still am about it and how it has been on my mind. (I was all ears, hesitant to say anything, still hurt and disappointed and yes, wounded, by the memory after our time in Mexico in 1974.) I thought we both handled it well on the trip with Adventurers to Mexico in 1975, and just back to Brazil last year. It was all 'business' between us on those trips, as we agreed; hard to imagine now, the old cliché of 'just friends,' but the trips and the two years are done and over. I did make a promise to you, and I have not forgotten it. Will you give me a chance now and after our trip to make it up to you? I'm older, you're older, we both have two more years of seeing the world, adventure travel and the single life under our belts. I think that's what I really wanted, two more years of freedom. It isn't just young men who are afraid of losing their freedom you know. Was it all a mistake?"

"Amy, there's also another cliché that may pertain: you can't turn love on and off. It has been lonely out in Lincoln, I don't deny it. And I don't deny I was hoping maybe this time it would be different. But I'm scarred, if that's the right word, maybe hardened in the heart, and apprehensive. Is it like starting over? I don't know. It can't be; we know each other too well and have gone through too much together. I'm thinking of that summer of 1974 in Mexico and the Pyramid at Chichén - Itzá. And all those terrific days and nights we were together; I thought I would never meet or have someone like you. I was in paradise the whole time. Then, like a Bronx cheer! The air went out of the balloon. You don't know how difficult it was to be back on those last two trips with you just as a 'friend.'"

Amy got up, came over and sat on my lap, looked into my eyes with those green eyes, tears running down her face. What does a guy do? I can't stand to see women cry, but especially this woman. I just held her, she turned and we exchanged warm kisses and hugs. I said, "Amy you've got to give me a little more room and I think you know why." She laughed then, smiled and said, "That's the plan, see if our chemistry is still good." It was so it seemed. We made another agreement – something like a revisit to those times on "Adventurer" the first time in Brazil. Romance on our time off. I said I thought my scars would take a long time to heal; she said she would make it happen. And I didn't mean the obsidian knife scar from Chichén.

So the end of that first encounter was an agreement to see how the next three weeks on board and my dream places for two more weeks (and hers too but maybe to a lesser extent, after all I was the Ph.D. in Spanish Golden Age Literature with a minor in Luso – Brazilian Studies) in romantic Portugal and Spain would treat us. Amy said we would be an "item" again on "Adventurer," and she could handle that. As long as we were "cool" about it, good friends and colleagues in public and closer friends during some secret rendezvous after hours. Harry Downing of old IA's trip around Brazil back in 1973 was boss this time and could keep a secret. We agreed to meet at the Charter Room, sit together and be "cool."

I was too excited for a nap in spite of the overnight flight, so I did a long shower, shaved and put on clean clothes, AT attire at that. I knew the way to the Chart Room, now my third trip on "Adventurer" but still nervous to be with the amazing people. There was a bit of melee, loud talking, old friends greeting each other. But the first to come up to me was Harry Downing the IAL [International Adventurer Leader] for this trip. He gave me a proper English hand shake, a light embrace and that old Oxford smile.

"Not much time to chat now Michael, but I want you to know I am really glad you are joining us. I'm going to work you hard, but will be at your side should any difficulties come up. You are our 'main man' for the on-board culture to come and prepping for the shore excursions. I'm always around to take the edges off your unbridled appreciation for Catholic Portugal and Spain. Remember King Henry the VIII, the Church of England, 1588 and the Armada! (He laughed long and hard.) But no one like you for accuracy and enthusiasm, just what AT envisions for our Adventurers. I'm hoping we can have a short private meeting tonight after dinner for the trip strategy, much of which I have already planned but needing your finishing touches. We'll have all day at sea tomorrow for you to give a talk, an Introduction to Portugal and Lisbon. Check with Amy for the on-shore options for Lisbon."

I returned the greeting telling ole' Harry I was simply pleased to be in his august presence! We both laughed. There was some socializing with staff, many I knew from the two former trips, and then a fine "Adventurer" first lunch. Adventurers were still coming on board through the afternoon. I would have time to make some notes on Lisbon for them. But Amy and I did squeeze a two-hour quick tour of downtown Funchal. We saw the incredible fish and flower market and walked to the old historic plaza where I insisted we see the Jesuit Church. It was astounding to me, gold gilt, beautiful azulejos, and the statue of dedication to Francisco Xavier the second in line Jesuit after Ignacio de Loyola and the number one missionary to the Far East, India, China and especially Japan. Along with Simon Rodrigues, he would be the most important Jesuit for Portugal.

There was a baptism going on and I could hear the local priest doing the officiating and then the famous (to me) Portuguese i.d. the "cãããã" ["uuuh" in English] instead of the "pois" in Brazil which always made me laugh. I couldn't help but stop to say hello to a priest in dress blacks, white collar and East Indian appearance. He was like us, a tourist. Most amazing he said he would soon be departing Madeira on the "International Adventurer" to Lisbon, the rest of Portugal and Spain. We laughed, introduced ourselves and said we would see him on board later in the p.m.

After our return to the ship I spent the rest of the afternoon making notes for the introduction to Lisbon. This would be my only night in Madeira, but you take what you can get. IA had scheduled an evening out in Funchal. The ride from the port up to the restaurant high on the hills to the side of the sea was beautiful – vineyard after vineyard, spectacular views of Funchal below, the gorgeous sunset on the water. The dinner was intentionally the "flavor of Madeira" - that Madeira beef specialty on a spit, wonderful fresh and flavorful tomato and lettuce salad, Portuguese potatoes, and flan for dessert, and of course Portuguese wines and then sweet Madeira after the meal (I can't help it, "Have Some Madeira My Dear;" I would sing that bawdy song aboard ship later on the trip); then we were in vans back to the ship. I had sat with Amy, Harry and Eli Hamilton our musical wizard, not yet introduced to our adventurers but known to most. The instrumental Madeiran music during dinner was to my taste with Portuguese "guitarradas," but not understanding one word of the lyrics. And I regret to say, I would not be able to see the sights on this fertile, garden island. And one of the best whaling museums in the world. Maybe some other time. Many adventurers had seen it all, and Harry Downing said he should be honorary mayor for the nearly two dozen times he had led AT tours here in Funchal.

Back aboard Harry asked me to come to his cabin for a nightcap (remember he's British, whiskey straight, no ice!). It was that chat that put me a bit on edge, not that he intended to frighten me, but just wanted me to be clued in of what might come.

"Mike, you know your Peninsular history and that both Portugal and Spain are really coming out of very bad in fact dismal economic times dating from World War II and the continuation of the Salazar and Franco regimes. Both countries have realized the importance of the tourist dollar and are encouraging the industry, so that's the good news. The bad news is that there really is sporadic unrest, the carryover from the "Revolution of the Flowers" in Portugal in 1974 and Franco's death in Spain in 1975. I assume you are familiar with what has been going on.

"Portugal was turned upside down mainly with the final and popular end (for most Portuguese) of the interminable land war in trying to maintain the former colonies. Lives and national wealth (and there is not much of the latter) were wasted in years of trying to maintain Portuguese hegemony. (England was smarter; we maintained the Commonwealth, uh, except the States, but that's another story.) Angola, Mozambique,

Guiné – Bissau and Cabo Verde all lost. And a few hundred thousand refugees came to the mainland living in poverty and trying to scratch out a living. Salazar is dead and gone (God rest his weary soul) but there has been a backlash to the largely socialist bent of 1974.

"Spain is the same but different (as are their collective personalities as you well know). In a way it's much more challenging. Black and white. The totalitarian repressive Franco regime since 1939, the Catholic Church the only church, and cronyism and favoritism to Franco imploded. Thank god King Juan Carlos Borbón is a rational man, willing to be creative and flexible and sharing the power with a Constitutional Monarchy now in 1977. But he's not home free; a good portion of Spain has not moved on, wants Franco to come out of his grave and keep the noose tightened on the anarchists, socialists, communists, and oh yes, all the old Republicans and the frosting on the cake, the Basque Separatists. But, blimey, you would never know it by all the tourism crowd – the hotels, the restaurants, the flamenco halls, and the rest. And the castles don't care. We mainly have to keep our eyes open and ears to the ground; the old, beautiful Spain you studied is still there, but you may have to use a bit of tunnel vision to see it.

"We have a handful of guests on board with close ties to either country, as might be expected, even some nobility, and an interesting Catholic Priest from Goa. (I interjected we already met him at the Jesuit Church in town. He said 'It takes one to know one, the Catholics I mean. Ha ha.') I'll look forward to reports from you after meeting them; we appreciate your language and cultural expertise. It should all come in handy. And I see the Peixotos from Brazil are back on board (the retired Itamarati Diplomats); you should get a bonus for that, they asked about you before signing up."

"Thanks Harry, all understood. Full speed ahead. This is a dream come true for me."

We all were tucked in and IA departed Madeira around midnight, all looking forward to that next day ahead, our first "at sea" and all to come.

2

AT SEA FROM MADEIRA
TO LISBON

The next morning birders were on the bridge with Jack and Kelly and Willy as well (naturalists from many IT trips and familiar to me from Brazil). It should be noted that we were in the very waters where the largest whaling industry ever created prospered for years, and many whales still roam the waters. At 10:00 a.m. Harry would do an introductory talk on the entire trip emphasizing the history, grandeur and times to come. At 2:00 p.m. I was scheduled for the introductory talk prepping all for the arrival in Lisbon and treats to come. Here it is:

MIKE'S FIRST TALK ON PORTUGAL AND
LISBON AND THEIR HISTORY

"Metropolitan Lisbon has over three million in population and the old city center has some 550,000. It is the westernmost large city located in Europe lying on the western Iberian Peninsula on the Atlantic Ocean and the River Tagus. An interesting tourist note is that it is the seventh-most-visited city in Southern Europe after Istanbul, Rome, Barcelona, Madrid, Athens and Milan. I understand that it is the oldest city in Western Europe predating London and Paris by hundreds of years. Julius Caesar made it a "municipium;" he named it "Olissipo." After the fall of Rome, it was ruled by Germanic tribes from the 5th century, captured by the Moors in the 8th century and was reconquered by Bergundian King Affonso Henriques and the Crusaders in 1147. The city grew as Portugal's capital and as the Portuguese expeditions of the Age of Discovery left from Lisbon during the 15th to 17th centuries. The 15th and 16th centuries were its "Golden Age" with discovery and commerce in Africa, India, and the Far East and later on Brazil. The Manueline style of architecture of that period predominated in the Tower of Belem and the Jerónimos Monastery.

"After the debacle of young King Sebastian and his utopic battle against the Moors in Morocco and his subsequent death in 1578, the crown was left vacant and in the succession crisis Spain came to rule in 1580. The Restoration took place sixty years later in 1640 with the Avis Dynasty in place. The House of Avis continued its rule until the earth shattering, literally, earthquake of 1755 which destroyed a large part of Lisbon. It would be rebuilt by Sebastião José de Carvalho e Melo, the 1st Marquis of Pombal.

"The next important time was the invasion of Portugal by Napoleon Bonaparte in the 19th century forcing the Bragança Queen Maria I and Prince-Regent João VI to flee with the royal family to Brazil. This is the only time in modern history of Europe when the home country is ruled from its colony! After Napoleon's defeat the royal family returned, minus Pedro I who decided to remain in Brazil. Brazilianists recall his "I am staying" ["Eu fico"] speech and established a constitutional monarchy there until the forced abdication of the Braganças in 1889.

"The Braganças then ruled in Portugal until 1908 with the regicide of Carlos I and the advent of the First Republic.

"The next great moment was the "Estado Novo" of much of the twentieth century under Antônio Salazar and his death followed by the Revolution of the Flowers in 1974 and its turmoil now, bringing the Portuguese Third Republic.

"There are ties to some of Europe's best Renaissance literature with Luís de Camões and his epic poem 'The Lusiads,' and we shall see the famous Portuguese "azulejos" and taste the best of its wines. It is no accident that the oldest political alliance in Europe is from 1386 between Portugal and England, and that Port Wine is its largest export to England and furthermore, droves of English tourists inundate Portugal's coastal towns and beaches in summertime.

"Here's what we will see tomorrow; you will have a lot on your plate.

A.M.
"A Praça dos Libertadores"
"Monumento ao Marquês de Pombal"
"Rossio, a Estação dos Trens"
View of "Rio Tejo" and "Praça do Comércio"
Blue Tile "Azulejos" – Old Scene of "Praça do Comércio"
Shopping in the "Chiado" District

Lunch on Board

P.M. "Castelo de São Jorge"
"Museu dos Azulejos"
"O Elétrico" (option 1). Meet others in evening at Fado Restaurant.
"Igreja da Sé" (option 2).
"Bairro Alto" (A Brazileira)

"We'll end the day with dinner and Fado Music in the Bairro Alto. We will have guides all along the way and I'll only speak up if there is a language difficulty (probably mine) or a question on your part."

Later that afternoon, at 5:30 p.m. we are still at sea from Madeira. CC (Chat and Cocktails, an AT tradition) would not begin tonight, but there would be a gathering in the lounge for Harry to introduce staff and Captain Tony's ship crew. Now a "veteran," albeit still a learner on AT travel and now a third time on "International Adventurer," IA from now on, I was used to the "drill." Harry Downing began, introducing Amy, myself, Jack, Kelly, Willy, and Eli. It was a reunion of old timers from the first trip to Brazil - Jack Bataldi on spotting birds, Kelly Corrigan with flora and fauna of the Peninsula, and yes, old favorite Willie Walsh for sea life around the peninsula. Willy in a private aside to me got to the "quick," saying he was sorry that Amy would be unavailable for the naturalists' flirting, well maybe not. And Eli Hamilton was aboard to do the music on ship and on shore, a treasure to come.

Then Captain Tony did the same with his crew, Exec Martim Mendes, Hotel Manager Gino Amato, Purser Joana Oliveira, Chef Reynaldo Romano, and Mr. Wong (Chinese but with a gorgeous Thai wife in charge of the female service crew) the head of the Thai on – board people. There was a full contingent of adventurers, 104 in total, and probably one – third had been on previous expeditions which I was on - among others "grouchy lady," and Wonky the come what may, careless camera wizard. It was terrific to have, once again, Leonel Peixoto the retired Itamarati Diplomat with wife Uíara and four colleagues (he said the 1973 trip around Brazil was so pleasant, especially his appreciation for IA staff and my work in particular, that he wanted to add to the retirement experience with his own return to the Peninsula). I gave him a big Brazilian "abraço" telling him how pleased that made me and that this time I would be occasionally asking for some advice for my talks, explaining that Portugal and Spain were academic specialties but without in – country experience. We agreed to sit together for that first dinner after the intro to Lisbon.

That was fun, much talk of "old times" on the "Adventurer" in 1973. I related that all went well, that we added Curitiba and the Morretes Train in 1976; he laughed at that, "Que calhambeque! [What a jalopy!]. Did you see anything?" I said we couldn't see the forest for the trees, but I did spy one Toucan. And the beef and shrimp and icy beer in Morretes were worth the three hours of boredom on the train, and added I was not interested in doing it again. But that the bus terminals and tubes in Curitiba were amazing. He added that he knew that famous mayor Jaime Lerner and if everyone in Brazil were like that, the country would be better off. I asked what news from his end? He said, "It's a good time to be retired; you'll notice I have a good tan and the belt line is stretched from good food and drink. Uíara is fine as you see, but lack of freedom in Brazil right now have not improved and we just hope for better times. But, 'porra,' it's good to see you. We are 'matando saudades' ['reliving old times'] in Portugal and Spain; I served in both countries and what changes! Salazar's death, the Revolution of the Flowers and events in Spain. I'll tell you more later. But how's your love life? I recall Amy and you were 'mandando brasa' ['getting it on'] on the '73 trip."

"Leonel, we still are still good friends and colleagues now on this trip, but there's a whole new story of escapades in Mexico in 1974 and 1975. I'll fill you in later about that. It got a bit dicey! There's a new book all about it."

Uíara spoke up, "You know 'arretado' ('cool guy' - Chico Buarque de Hollanda's nickname for me back in 1971 escapades) has an eye for women, including several in Brazil, but I think I can match those chicks in a 'fio dental.' Ha." She looked at me and winked. I think I blushed a bit, but gave her a quick kiss. Suspicions confirmed. I'm sure the Brazilians had a good idea of what was and is going on with Amy and me. Hopefully AT and IA would not get upset for a small kiss among friends.

After dinner Eli Hamilton gives a fine introduction to the music of Portugal, emphasizing the "fado" and explaining the instruments, the music tradition, and a fine video of Amália Rodrigues and her famous song "Uma Casa Portuguesa."

Amy and I have a short get together in her room, drinks like old times and some spooning. Both excited for what is ahead.

3

FIRST A.M. AND DAY IN LISBON

We arrived in Lisbon early dawn, sun streaming through just a few clouds, all brilliantly colored for a moment. It's "Springtime in Portugal." Many adventurers were out on deck as "Adventurer" entered the Tagus [Rio Tejo] estuary and then the river proper. On the left was the wharf of Cascais with the shiny buildings reflecting the sun and houses up above, then we slowly drifted by Belém (its entire history based on the age of Discovery in the late 15th and early 16 centuries; the caravels left from here on the famous voyages), the ship at low speed on orders from Captain Tony. We would visit this spectacular area in a day or two, the Mosteiro [Monastery] de Belém, the modern huge monument to the Discoverers, the Tower of Belém (a 16th century fortification), the April 25th Bridge across the Tejo and finally the dock itself.

Praça de Commércio e o Rio Tejo

We were down the way from the famous and main "Praça de Commércio" or "Praça do Paço" (Plaza of Commerce and of the Palace respectively) but you could see the buildings of old Lisbon straight ahead, the Bairro Alto to the left and the outline of the "Castelo de São Jorge" to the right, all on our busy excursion schedule. As "Adventurer" eased into its birth at the docks there was one down note: signs painted in red by the dock workers' union protesting the fact that our service crew was Thai and not Portuguese. "Adventurer" after all was built in O Porto, staffed by a Portuguese captain and his crew, so why not the service crew? A good question. The protest was peaceable but caught the attention of all of us. Captain Tony said he would address the issue in a soon to be CC on board.

All of us had a good breakfast on board and were "equipped" with water bottles, cameras, and documents and met our local guides at the bottom of the stairway to the dock. All the excursion vans would go to the same destinations but at different times but not "reporting" until our CC tomorrow night. The guides were supposedly bilingual and we discovered all had "King's English" rather than American accents. Harry Downing would comment on this at CC reminding all that the oldest diplomatic treaty in all

Europe dated back to 1386, the Treaty of Windsor, between Portugal and England. And that England was the number one customer of Portuguese wines and Portuguese tourism. Much more on this as we moved along on the trip. There were however many occasions when the guides' English lacked a term or two and yours truly had to step in for "clarification."

This was a very dicey and tricky situation; the guides had their own union, were especially proud of their knowledge, expertise and language abilities. In fact, I noted what I surmised was a bit of "continental superiority" in the whole matter, not nearly as friendly, easy − going and cooperative as the guides we all experienced in Brazil, and Mexico for that matter. Old World − New World? Harry Downing was our expert on all this and would clarify a bit later on. I forgot to say he had warned me of it in our initial introductory talk in Madeira. Duly noted. My main role was aboard ship cultural preparation, and he advised a "low − key" approach on shore. I readily agreed and enthusiastically looked forward to my own "education" once on land.

Here's what happened that long first but delightful day in Lisbon.

"AVENIDA DA LIBERDADE"

Vans take us first to Lisbon's main avenue; I understand modeled after the main avenues of Paris; "Avenida da Liberdade" with its beautiful trees and cafés links the "Praça dos Restauradores" to the "Praça de Pombal." The avenue is broad with many lanes of traffic and long broad sidewalks with gardens along their sides. The avenue evolved from the "Passeio Público" from 1764; it soon had the palaces of the wealthiest families of Lisbon along its side. These have been replaced by office buildings, hotels and cinemas (we saw advertisements for a Charles Bronson adventure film), but still there are statues remembering the height of Portuguese literary history with figures of the age like Almeida Garrett, Alexandre Herculano, and others. It is the scene of the largest parade in Lisbon with the night of St. Anthony of Lisbon.

We were all walking at this point and it was a good thing. Everyone stretched their legs on Avenida da Liberdade with its nice walkways. Along the way we stopped for a Portuguese nicety, the "bica" or Portuguese version of the Brazilian "cafezinho." Strong, black, sugary and delicious! Leonel Peixoto was in my group and could not help but inform us all that Portugal owed it all to Minas Gerais and its "good" coffee, a topic we would learn more of later. Next on the huge avenue was an equally huge monument.

"MONUMENTO AO MARQUÊS DE POMBAL"

Pombal and the Lion

The monument is dedicated to the "Marquês de Pombal" Sebastião José de Carvalho e Melo, the prime minister who ruled Portugal from 1750 to 1777. He is most beloved by the Portuguese by virtue of rebuilding Lisbon after the devastating earthquake of 1755, justly so. But for me he was the leader of Portugal who among other things would reign at the time of the decree throwing the Jesuit Order out of Brazil and Spanish America as well in 1767. Without some serious research and many pages of prose, horribly involved stuff, one cannot know the whys and wherefores of all this. But for the Brazilians and "Brazilianists" and people who admire the Jesuits, he gets a black mark. From the times of Padre Antônio Vieira who preached to the indigenous natives in Northeastern Brazil, to the Jesuit who wrote the first Portuguese Grammar Book in Brazil, to the countless Jesuits who brought Christianity to the natives of Brazil, in particular, to the "Missões" in the South, all was lost with Pombal's decree. The Order had to leave the premises, almost, as it were, "overnight." Schools, hospitals and missions were left to the Crown to designate to other religious orders. It took a long while for Brazil to recover. One needs to see the film "The Mission" with Robert de Niro and Jeremy Irons to get an idea of the devastating consequences for the natives of southern Brazil, albeit with touches of Hollywood. The Jesuits were allowed to return in a most modest fashion, and with the Second Vatican Council and its aftermath, play a much different role in today's Brazil. They espoused the "Preference for the Poor" and much of the theology of Liberation Theology and are champions of the cause of poor Brazilians yet today.

We then walked a way to the Rossio Train Station with its Manueline architectural style and past "Restauradores" ["Restorers"] Monument marking Portugal's independence from Spain in 1640. We recall once again that Spain came to rule Portugal in 1580 as a consequence of the death of Portuguese King Sebastião of the House of Avis who had embarked on a utopist mission to carry the conquest of the Moors from Portugal into northern Africa where he met his end. But the year of 1640 brought an end that was not so clear cut; Portugal and Spain were at each other's throats for many years, but the culmination was the rule of the House of Bragança until the 20th century and the end of it all.

Rossio Plaza is the main transportation hub of Lisbon with the trains heading out to all corners of Portugal. One of the main squares of Lisbon since the Middle Ages, it is a center of popular life in Lisbon as well as its Rossio Train Station. It was the place of the Portuguese Inquisition and there were public executions in the plaza in the 16th Century. Two centuries later after the earthquake in 1755 the Romantic writer Almeida Garrett convinced all to build the Portuguese National Theater where the Inquisition building had been destroyed, the Teatro Maria Isabel. But back in the 16th century it later had been a meeting place for the Portuguese to conspire against Spain and its control of Portugal from 1580 (as noted, King Sebastião was killed in Morocco and with no hereditary leader, by blood it all passed to Spain and Felipe II) to 1640 and the famous Restoration. As mentioned, our practical connection to the Square was the Rossio Train Station which was built in 1886 in Neo-Manueline Architecture. On that enormous first day in Lisbon it was difficult to absorb it all; it felt like when I landed as a young bachelor set to do Ph.D. research in Rio de Janeiro in 1966 and was overwhelmed by the immensity of the city.

The Rossio Train Station was jammed with huge crowds of commuters to the suburbs. This was the main railroad station of Lisbon of the Portuguese Royal Railway Company from 1886 to 1988, built on Rossio Square and connecting the city, among other places, to Sintra. Service was restricted to a few long service lines when IA was there. It was built in the "Neo - Manueline" style typical of early 16th century Portugal. (We shall talk at length of King Manoel and the architectural style attributed to him once we visit Belém in a day or two.) One notices the two intertwined horseshoe portals at the entrance. Inside there are ramps connecting to a cast-iron structure. Trains gain access to the station through a tunnel more than 2600 meters long. I surmised it should be an easy train ride to our destination of Sintra on another day. Oops, that would be a smaller electric train on the other side of town.

Then it was back to old Lisbon overlooking the Rio Tejo. We saw the spectacular view of the "Rio Tejo" and "Praça do Commércio." While serenely gazing down to the river we noted several men of very poor appearance up to their knees in the mud digging large worms for fishing bait ["gusanos de isca"]. The tide was out and there was a foul smell close to the water. The overflowing worm buckets were a bit disgusting that first morning in Lisbon.

Then it was down to the main plaza of old Lisbon and its blue tile "Azulejos" depicting the old scene of the "Praça do Commércio." On the way down the hill we walked through the busy commercial center of Lisbon on the "mosaic sidewalks" like those in Rio. The "Praça do Commércio" or "A Praça do Paço" faced the famous and impressive Tagus River with the huge 25th of April Bridge (renamed after the 1974 Revolution) to the right or north and a Christ figure across the river. The river and docks were replete with large ocean liners, navy and cargo ships and many ferries. Originally known as the "Terreiro do Paço" or Palace Square because it was the place of the Royal Ribeira Palace, it was later to be destroyed in the earthquake of 1755 and rebuilt as the "Praça do Commércio" by the Marquês de Pombal. It had been King Manuel of the Avis Dynasty who had built the Ribeira Palace in the early 16th century (the time of the "Manuelino" architecture throughout Lisbon and Belém). The original plaza had housed the "Casa da Índia" regulating commerce with that part of the world after the discoveries of Vasco da Gama in 1497 (related to the similar purpose of the "Casa de Contratación" of Spain in Sevilla). It contains a great arch and a statue of a Portuguese King in Lisbon which highlights the Praça. A gloomier fact is that it also was the place where the next to last King of Portugal, Carlos I, was assassinated in 1908. Only two years later the Republicans overthrew the Portuguese monarchy.

From there it was just a short walk to the main shopping area of old Lisbon's port. This part of Lisbon has been inhabited since Roman times! North European Crusaders later settled in the area during the Siege of Lisbon in 1147 to retake Portugal from the Moors. Prosperity followed and then disaster; the 1755 earthquake luckily did only minimal damage. Adventurers were now tired and a bit hungry so it was back to the ship for lunch.

LUNCH ON BOARD
P.M.

That afternoon of the first day. There is continuing delightful spring weather, a bit cool but with sunshine. Then it was off to the "Castelo de São Jorge."

"O CASTELO DE SÃO JORGE" - HISTORY

The vans and guide took us to the "Castelo de São Jorge" one of the landmarks of Lisbon. It was my first European castle! From the parapet one has a fine view of the Rio Tejo, the Alfama district and the rest of the city. Its history is amazing. It was originally a Moorish castle occupying a hilltop overlooking the old historic center of Lisbon and the Tagus River. Prior to that time it had roots in Celtic tribes, Phoenicians, Greeks, Carthaginians and the Romans. With the fall of Rome, the "Suevos" and Visigoths ruled before the Moors. With the Christian "Reconquista" by Affonso Henriques and the Knights of the Second Crusade the siege of Lisbon took place in 1147 and the Christians took Lisbon. The Castle was later named "São Jorge" after the Pact with the English in 1376. The latter were important allies of the Portuguese in 1385 and the Battle of Aljubarrota in effect freeing Portugal from Spanish dominion. Once again, we were told this is the oldest political alliance in Europe. When Lisbon became the center of the Kingdom in 1255, the Castelo de São Jorge became the fortified residence of King Afonso III, was later renovated by King Dinis in 1300 and became the Royal Palace of the Alcáçova. The castle resisted the advances of Spain in the 14th century and was finally dedicated to King João I and his wife Filipa of Lancaster. Later the castle was the setting for the reception of the return of Vasco da Gama from India in 1498. It was a theater for the plays of Gil Vicente, Portugal's most famous playwright. It began its decline in the 16th century when the Portuguese built a new palace along the Tagus River in Belém, a "suburb" of Lisbon along the Tagus reaching to the open Atlantic. The decline continued during the Spanish rule and finally with much destruction by the earthquake of 1755. Salazar in the 20th century sponsored its rebuilding and it is a major tourist site today.

After the castle there was a walk through the "Alfama."

Street in the Alfama

It is the oldest district of Lisbon, between the "Castelo de São Jorge" and the "Rio Tejo." The name comes from the Arabic "fountains or baths." During the time of the Moors it constituted the entire city of Lisbon; it later became the main aristocratic part of the city, but much later was inhabited by the fishermen and other poor "Lisboetas" and remains that way today. It escaped the earthquake of 1755 so remains largely intact. The "miradouros" or overlooks to the Tagus are impressive as is the nearby beginning of the Lisbon trolley or "elétrico" and the Museum of Portuguese Tiles or "Azulejos."

Since many buildings of the "Alfama" were not affected by the horrendous earthquake of 1755, it appears very old. From the nearby Belvedere of the "Largo de São Salvador" we saw once again the view of the river and beyond. The streets are cobblestone and the sidewalks are "pedradas," stones smooth from wear and slippery. Some of IA's elderly adventurers had to take it extraordinarily slow using their walking sticks to traverse the area. The Alfama was all very quaint with narrow winding streets and lots of "becos" or dead end alleyways as well. The balconies were replete with flowers and the streets with lots of stray dogs. It had more character than some other parts of the city, and yet the latter were not far behind. The famous balconies all had the laundry out, a trait of the Alfama.

Our guide warned of street thieves in the Alfama, but one shop owner said the thieves "get only little old women." Yet it happened; a thief bumped into one of the elderly adventurers and grabbed her handbag. Lisbon being what it is, very huge, that was the last of that. A real "downer" yet what can you do? She fortunately had only xerox copies of her documents (as recommended by AT) and limited cash, but was shaken by the experience. But she insisted on finishing the outing, a real trooper!

There were many typical cafés, and some "tascas" or bars. We did see one or two "varinas," the fish monger ladies dressed all in black with boots on and busy cleaning fish. There were one or two "fado" restaurants but I understand the "Bairro Alto" is better known for this. The Alfama seemed almost free of cars and traffic, very nice. At its end we were back to the Belvedere overlooking the Rio Tejo and a few doors down was ...

THE "MUSEU DE AZULEJOS"

Adventurers could see this or go ahead and get on the Lisbon Trolley which stopped nearby. Portugal is most famous for these tiles which it took to its many colonies - possessions, including to Brazil (we saw them again just last year especially in the colonial churches of the Northeast, like the convents of Olinda or the "Igreja de São Francisco" in Salvador), so this had to be an important part of Lisbon for me. The custom was inherited from the Moorish tradition but found a true home in Portugal where outstanding examples can be found throughout the nation. The museum itself was outstanding, a beautiful example of art and culture in Lisbon and Portugal.

Then getting on in the afternoon we walked to old downtown to the Cathedral of Lisbon [Igreja da Sé]. Its official name is "The Patriarchal Cathedral of St. Mary Major of Lisbon." It was begun by Afonso Henriques in 1147 after retaking Lisbon from the Moslems and has been modified many times hence. An English Crusader Gilbert of Hastings was named its first bishop and the church was built on the site of the first Mosque of Lisbon. King Dinis in the 13th century ordered a cloister to be built in the Gothic Style and it is in this place that we saw the Gothic Tomb of Knight Lopo Fernandes Pacheco, 7th Lord of Ferreira de Aves, in the ambulatory. His figure appears holding his sword and is guarded by a dog.

Since this is a 12th century church; it reminds from the outside of Notre Dame in Paris (from the pictures I have seen) and the "Igreja da Sé" in old Coimbra. (We will see the latter in a few days.) It was a fortress church in its beginnings. It is the oldest church in Lisbon and is of Romanesque and Gothic design. It was huge and cavernous with just a few stained - glass windows. There were Gothic niches with altars. Somewhere to the back of the main altar ["altar maior"] there were the sarcophagi of an archbishop of the 14th century and the knight already mentioned. The building all seemed a bit dingy, but is impressive for its size and the entrance.

There was the other event of that busy afternoon, an option for Adventurers: the Electric Trolley ["o Elétrico"] from the Alfama District. They would meet us all later in the Bairro Alto for the Brazileira Tea Room and the Fado Restaurant. The rest of us would go to the Cervejaria District just up the hill from the port. We enjoyed beers, wine and talk at the bar district (and ate snails with the help of needles). The adventurers chose the old international stand – by Matheus Rosé wine, but the guide at my insistence introduced them to one of the delights of Portuguese – "Vinho Verde," a light wine with just a touch of carbonation like champagne. It was a big hit.

Back to the "Elétrico" or famous Lisbon Trolley. My group did not take the trolley but it's important to write about it. The first tramway in Lisbon entered service in 1873 as a horse car line, but all was converted to electricity in 1901. The Lisbon Metro and the bus system have of course reduced its use and importance. But it remains one of the few in Europe. Debate as to its usefulness continues in Lisbon. You can get on at its starting point, the "Largo de São Miguel" and the "Chafariz de Baixo" looking down on the docks. If you do the entire route, it takes one and one half - hour ride and you see a lot of old Lisbon. The route starts at the east side of the "Baixa" in the city center and does a complete circle coming out at the "Chiado" at Carmo. Later on, adventurers told us they were struck by the density of the city and its crowds, but also by its apparent poverty in what seemed not slums but grey, old, worn business districts. The passersby seemed drab with rather plain dress. There was intense traffic and a seeming total lack of parking space and greenness almost the entire route. It made Lisbon appear huge with cars parked everywhere including at the principal plaza the "Paço."

In early evening we were back in the vans to the Bairro Alto with its view of the city. Built from the old city walls of Lisbon, it gradually developed in importance. The arrival of the Jesuits in 1540 and the establishment of São Roque Church was an important time. In modern times it became known for the "Fado" cafés, the Largo de Camões, Rua

Garret and the bar-restaurant "A Brazileira." This renowned place was a favorite among adventurers (much like the Confeitaria Colombo had been in Rio). This café-tea shop-bar-restaurant is one of the oldest and most famous cafés in the old quarter of Lisbon located at 120 Rua Garrett at one end of the Largo do Chiado near the Baixa-Chiado Metro Stop. It started in 1905 by selling "genuine Brazilian coffee" from the state of Minas Gerais. It was the first shop to sell the "bica", a small cup of strong coffee like Brazil's "cafezinho." It was at the "Brazileira" that most of us were introduced once again to the "bica." Its most famous client was the great 20th century poet Fernando Pessoa whose bronze statue is placed outside the place.

The fado restaurant offered Portuguese cuisine but also something quite basic - delicious Portuguese style barbecued chicken ["frango grelhado"]. Adventurers enjoyed once again delicious "Vinho Verde" or small glasses of that sweet and strong Port. The main event was the actual Fado performance. I've got to at least say a bit about that since it's so famous. There is perhaps just one name to remember for traditional "fado" of Lisbon: Amália Rodrigues, and one song, "Uma Casa Portuguesa." This is a huge simplification, but so be it. The truth is this: if you are not a Portuguese speaker and a "Lisboeta" at that, what fascinates you is the "fadista" dressed in black with the traditional black shawl, the male "fadista" in black suit to her side, the beautiful melodies, sometimes dark emphasizing once again the Portuguese cliché of "saudade" or intense melancholy. But you won't understand the Portuguese. It's the sound, the tone and especially the instrumental accompaniment of the Portuguese "guitarras" of 10 or 12 strings, the "viola" of 6 strings and a base guitar. But all acoustic, god forbid amplification. As an amateur classic guitarist and singer of "oldies" from U.S. country and folk music, and a smattering of Spanish and Brazilian "oldies," I loved to hear the "fado" and was mesmerized by those guitars. But once again, the lyrics. Just for our crowd Eli had printed out Amália's "Uma Casa Portuguesa" and I tried to translate it, and we of course requested it. Trouble is, they really did not take requests, but did do it after a special request (and tip) by Eli. Here are the lyrics:

> Numa casa Portuguesa fica bem; pão e vinho sobre a mesa;
>
> E se na porta humildemente bate alguém; sente -se à mesa com a gente;
>
> Fica bem esta fraquesa, fica bem; que o povo nunca desmente;
>
> A alegria desta pobreza está nesta grande riqueza; de dar e ficar contente.

Once you hear it, you can't forget it, one of those tunes that will forever stick in your head. That alone made the night a huge success. As we were leaving, one of the adventurers, an elegant and strikingly beautiful lady of perhaps thirty – five years of age came up to me, introduced herself as only Rachel. She said, "I hope I do not appear too forward, but could we sit together at lunch tomorrow in Cascais after the morning excursion to Belém.?" She spoke with a continental Portuguese accent but perfectly and precisely pronounced so that I got every word, "Senhor Gaherty, your fame precedes you. I have already talked to the Peixotos, old diplomatic friends from Brazil, and your love of the Portuguese language, Brazil and may I add Brazilian literature and music have been made known to me. And as well your connection to Chico Buarque de Holanda (I've been a fan for a long time and have all his recordings) has me really excited to meet you. I would love to perhaps enlighten you more about certain aspects of Portugal on this trip, facts not found in the history books, and perhaps we can begin tomorrow."

We on staff are encouraged to be with the adventurers, especially at meals, answer questions and just "be of help." I said, "Rachel, I think it is you not me that should be congratulated. Obrigado! You've got a date!" (I was not thinking of Amy.) She did ask about the girl sitting next to me at last night's dinner. Hmm.

Musing on that first day's experience after all the historic elements already mentioned, I wrote perhaps one or two less pleasing notes. Lisbon so far is historically more interesting than Rio, but appears old and poor with many street beggars. We noted all the graffiti along street walls, much of it by the P.C.P., "Partido Comunista Português," and we walked by the Socialist Party Headquarters. These things you did not see in Brazil. After the 1974 Revolution such divergent points of view became much more evident not only in Lisbon but all Portugal. As for the old and somewhat run – down buildings, there would be a very pleasant contrast and lesson on that the next day in Belém along the Tejo on the way to the open Atlantic Ocean.

I was pleased with the communicating in Portugal that first day, almost no problems at all with my Brazilian Portuguese. The Portuguese think I am from southern Brazil! The magic words "speak slowly please" ["fale devagar por favor"] solved most everything.

4

SECOND DAY IN LISBON

Adventurers took vans to the "Cais de Sodré" train station; there was much less city traffic than at Rossio Station and it was a quick trip. The former station however was in a poor area and reminded me of "Central do Brasil" in Rio. Yet, the commuter trains were electric, smooth and efficient. We traveled along the Rio Tejo for about fifteen minutes to Belém. Guides were with us the entire way including the rather intense next few hours in ...

BELÉM

Belém from the Portuguese word for "Bethlehem" is a civil parish in the municipality of Lisbon. It is six kilometers west of city center and two kilometers west of the Bridge "Ponte 25 de Abril." The area became famous for its military position along the mouth of the Tagus, its role in the exploration of India and the Orient (the "Caminho das Índias") and then royal residences like the Palácio de Ajuda. It is famous for several monuments.

Belém along the waterfront seemed old and a bit worse for wear, but up above the old part one could see there was a lot of new, shiny growth. It was evident that the middle and upper classes of greater Lisbon live outside the city center and the area of the trolley ride yesterday. Much of Belém seemed like Salvador's "orla" (the miles of beach and beach communities to the north of old Salvador) as compared to its old city. Cascais would confirm this view. Before tackling the monuments, we all stopped in a "confeitaria" nearby and had a nice "bica" and soft drink in a local café.

THE MONASTERY OF BELÉM ["O MOSTEIRO DE BELÉM"]

Jerônimos Monastery, Belém

The old hermitage on the spot was originally the home for the Hieronymite religious order <u>circa</u> 1459. It was originally administrated by monks of the religious-military Order of Christ. It was then enlarged and beautified into the great building it is today by King Manuel I and meant to be the resting place of the family members of the Casa dos Avis and as a church for seafaring adventurers who embarked during the Age of Discovery. In 1496 Manuel petitioned the Holy See to build the monastery at the entrance of Lisbon. Vasco da Gama and his men spent the night in prayer there at the older hermitage when departing for the Orient in 1497; upon his return in 1498 with samples of gold, it became a symbol and a house of prayer for seamen leaving the port.

Construction began again in 1501 and was completed 100 years later, the money coming from the five per cent tax on commerce from Africa and the Orient. Resources already planned for Batalha Monastery to the north of Lisbon (to be seen later) were transferred here. Boitaca was the original architect, then a Spaniard, the style thus moving from Portuguese Manueline to Spanish Plateresque. All halted with King Manuel's death in 1521.

Manel I had ordered the Hieronymite monks occupying the monastery to pray for his eternal soul and spiritual assistance for navigators and sailors who departed from the Bay of Reselo to discover the world.

Felipe II of Spain in 1604 made the Monastery a royal funerary monument. It was restored to Portugal in 1640.

Our guide's comments conflicted at times with the local literature on the places saying that in 1682 in the reign of Pedro II of Portugal the body of King Sebastian was buried in one of the transept chapels. This presents an historical problem: most accounts of history say King Sebastian's body was never recovered after the tragic battle in Morocco in 1578. However, according to some sources, King Felipe II of Spain claimed to recover the remains of the body of Sebastian and had him buried in Jerônimos. But this is not proven and is debated.

At any rate, Sebastian's tomb is at least a "symbolic" tomb recalling one of the great stories of Portuguese culture and history. Sorry, I've got to repeat, now for the third time, the story. In 1578 young King Sebastian took on the formidable task of carrying the conquest of the Moors to their own lands in Morocco but was soundly defeated and was killed at the battle of Alcáçar Quibir. They never found the body and there were amazing consequences. A legend arose about the person never found and that young, reckless Sebastian would return one day and lead tiny Portugal to days of greater glory. It never happened, but the legend was transferred to the backlands of northeastern Brazil and produced more than one "messianic" figure claiming either to be or to be inspired by Sebastian to "save" Brazil. The "Pedra Bonita" massacre of the early nineteenth century (1829) and the more famous War of Canudos (1896-1897) with the Messianic leader Antônio Conselheiro are cases in point. The latter became the subject of what some say is the Brazilian National Epic, "Os Sertões" ["Rebellion in the Backlands"] by the journalist-writer Euclides da Cunha. One noted that the tomb in Jerônimos was placed between marvelous carved elephants with tusks.

A literary aside. As a Brazilianist I have always had a problem with the exact literary role of "Os Sertões." First of all it is a work in prose, the result of the fieldnotes of the journalist Euclides da Cunha during the campaign of the war in 1896-1897. Does this disqualify it as being an Epic? I think so. Even then, many Brazilians call it "Brazil's greatest novel." I protest even more strongly here. The book is written in prose and is based on Da Cunha's diary reworked into a sociological and journalistic account of the times. In no way is it fiction or can resemble a novel. Case closed. A great work and really important in the evolution of Brazilian literature, an Epic in the European sense (in verse and in ten "cantos) it is not. Perhaps I protest too much, but after all these years of study in the academy it was good to get it off my chest. There is a relation to Sebastianism however with the role of Antônio Conselheiro.

There was much more to see in yet another chapel of the monastery of the "Jerônimos." In 1898, the 400th anniversary of the arrival of Vasco da Gama in India, they restored his tomb in "Jerônimos." One might recall that it was the Portuguese seafarers who first gained glory in the time of Christopher Columbus but prior to the later Spanish explorers one-half century later, a fact Portugal constantly reminds the world (and the Spanish).

Da Gama the seafarer left Lisbon and Belém in 1497 and arrived on the coast of India in 1498, this after descending the west coast of Africa, rounding the cape of Good Hope, encountering Moslem pirates on the east coast of Africa (20th century pirates encountered recently already existed even then!) and braved fierce storms to finally arrive in Goa on the west coast of India. He actually did a return trip four years later but it was the first that marked world history. No longer having to face the Moslem perils of the eastern Mediterranean or the Red Sea, Portugal opened up a true age of discovery in the Far East, including the Malaccas (near today's Indonesia), the coast of China and eventually Japan. The treasures were the spices so highly valued in Europe at the time. And a related topic would be the adventures of the Jesuit Missionaries, among them Mateo Ricci and Francisco Xavier to China and Japan. Da Gama's great exploit would be the moving force and primary topic of the Portuguese national epic, "The Lusiads" by Luís de Camões.

One of our adventurers was particularly interested in this, Jesuit Father Siqueiros from Goa in India. I would sit with him that night back on-board IA after CC at dinner.

Tomb of Luís de Camões

In the same chapel as Da Gama's tomb was the tomb of one of his greatest admirers, Luís de Camões, Portugal's most famous writer who wrote the Portuguese epic poem "The Lusiads" ["Os Lusíadas"] in the early 16th century. Camões was one of the reasons I wanted to participate on AT's trip to see Portugal (and then Spain). I had a wonderful reading of the poem in graduate school at Georgetown under the tutelage of Dr. Dolores Deemer who also introduced us to the highlights of Brazilian Literature. It is the dream of every professor of Portuguese Literature to have the opportunity to teach the master work in a graduate reading course.

The poem is a true epic poem in octaves and tells the tale of the great Portuguese voyages of discovery to the Far East in the 15th century. It is a

Renaissance version of the epic verse form and Camões had no qualms about basing much of its style on Virgil's "Aeneid" which of course in turn borrowed heavily from the "Iliad" and "Odyssey" of Homer and the Greek epic tradition. The poem in ten "cantos" placed tiny Portugal on the literary map of Europe. One also notes that Camões and this epic poem are the trademarks of Portuguese high culture in the academy. In fact the Portuguese language came to be called "the Language of Camões."

Camões' life is an epic as well. I think there are real parallels with Cervantes in Spain. With privileged parents he was able to study with the Dominicans and the Jesuits, and although perhaps not enrolled, spent significant time at the University of Coimbra. He lost an eye after serving as a soldier at the Battle of Ceuta in Africa in the 1500s. But what most changed him was the military and bureaucratic service in long years in the Far East, eventually as a bureaucrat in Macau with the unpleasant task of dealing with recovery of goods of the deceased Portuguese and their return to Portugal. He was not impressed by the level of honesty in general in such days. He was involved in shipwrecks, battles with Muslims, pirates and the like. After writing his masterpiece during this time in the far East based on the Vasco da Gama voyage (one legend is that he almost lost it in a shipwreck near the Mekong Delta and actually swam to shore with it in his hand!), and returning home to Portugal and short-lived literary fame, he experienced the low point of Portuguese history of the times, the news of the loss by Portugal to the Moors in 1578 in the Battle of Alcácer Quibir (today's Morocco) and the death of the young King Sebastião. Worse was that this left the Portuguese throne open to Spain's Felipe II by virtue of royal marriage and blood lines. Portugal had long ago (1385) battled to be independent from Spain and this brought a new nightmare to patriots, among the greatest Camões himself. He in fact died at the beginning of the Spanish domination in 1580.

Yours truly knelt before both tombs of Vasco da Gama and Camões in homage to these great men studied in the graduate courses at Georgetown University years ago. Not being so sure about King Sebastian's, I just marveled at the elephants with tusks in front of the marble "edifice." I think some adventurer saw this and got a laugh out of it plus a picture he showed me later. It was Wonky.

The cloister and fountains were equally impressive, all in the Manueline style. The style was actually given its name by Count Varnhagen in 1842 when writing about the style of the "Mosteiro de Belém." It refers to the king of the time when the architectue was so used, King Manuel I ("Casa dos Avis"). The style is linked to "Jerônimos" and influence from the time of Portuguese discoveries from Africa to the Far East. Short-lived from 1490 to 1520, it was seen in churches, monasteries, palaces and castles. Some say it combines late Gothic with Spanish Plateresque, "Mudéjar," and Italian and Flemish architecture. Themes are from the people, fauna and flora of the voyages of discovery and the Far East.

THE TOWER OF BELÉM ["A TORRE DE BELÉM"]

The Tower of Belém

The tower, really a fort, was constructed by King João II as part of a defensive system to protect access to the Tagus estuary. Originally called the "Tower of São Vicente," it was finished by Manuel I of Portugal (1515-1520) to guard the entrance to the port at Belém. And of course the architecture is "Manuelina." It is interesting to know that the Portuguese accompanied the construction of the actual tower with a "second team," a huge ship anchored nearby to defend the entrance to Lisbon, the "Grande Nau" of 1100 tons.

Over the succeeding years the Tower was used as fortress, dungeon, custom house, and even lighthouse along the Tejo. The Tower dates from the same period as the Monastery. It was from this point that the caravels left for Africa, Asia and America. It was very interesting with a stone block tower, winding stairway and turrets, a beautiful setting by the river.

THE MONUMENT TO THE DISCOVERERS ["MONUMENTO DOS DESCOBRIDORES"]

Monument of the Discovers

This is a 52-meter-high slab of concrete, erected in 1960 to commemorate the 500th anniversary of the death of Prince Henry the Navigator (we shall talk of him later). One may recall that it was Portugal in the 15th century that developed many of the mainstays of ocean travel in those unchartered times, among them the invention of the "Caravel" ship and sails which allowed tacking into the wind. It was on such ships with the help of the astrolabe for sighting stars that Portugal came to dominate the seven seas. It was sculpted in the form of a caravel ship's prow with dozens of figures from Portuguese history ascending to a statue of the "Infante" Henry the Navigator, all sculpted in base relief. Adjacent to the monument is a "calçada" or square in the form of a map, showing the routes of various Portuguese explorers from the Age of Discovery. And right across the street was yet another important memory from the great days of Portugal's past.

THE "MUSEU DOS COCHES"

Finally, and most of us were tired and hungry by now, the guide insisted we see one more thing – the Royal Carriage Museum. The nobility had to get around in those days, and this museum has many fine examples of the old "diligencias" or "stagecoaches." It is interesting to know that the museum is housed in the old horse-riding arena of the Belém Palace, now the official residence of the President of Portugal. The Museum was begun by Queen Amélia in 1905 and has samples from the 16th to the 19th centuries, among them the traveling coach of King Philip II of Portugal (Felipe II of Spain) used for travel from Spain to Portugal in 1619. Several of the coaches are related to the Vatican, either donated to the Portuguese Crown or used by the Portuguese Ambassador to the Vatican in the 18th century. Enough history and tourism for a while.

CASCAIS

Then vans took us all for a very late lunch to Cascais and the beaches, farther west on the coast from Belém. The town was originally connected to the administration of Sintra, but became an important fishing village and supplier for Lisbon in the 13th and 14th centuries. One of the most interesting facets of its history was during World War II when it became the home of many of the exiled royal families of Europe fleeing from the Fascist threat of World War II (Portugal remained neutral in it all, an amazing turn of events). And a very large number of Jewish refugees from Eastern Europe! It was a modern tourist town, complete with casino, "plaza de toros," and such for the modern tourists.

Adventurers were given free time. Some went to the local restaurants, some to the glitzy commercial area on hill beyond the port, some to Cascais's infamous casino (think early James Bond) and none to a Portuguese bull fight that afternoon. I will not talk in depth of the latter but it's a "hoot" for traditional Spanish bull fight aficionados! I've never seen one Portuguese style, but it's famous for fighting on horseback ("os cavaleiros"), fighting with a group of eight courageous,?, men rushing to grab the horns of the bull (often filed down in Portugal) and haul it down ("os forcados"). I've never seen rugby either, but is this a Portuguese "scrum?" And there are lady fighters too. The bull survives for the butcher shop or if courageous, for breeding. No one from IA attended, maybe a lack of tickets on spur of the moment, or maybe lack of interest. Ha. But the real "corrida" in Spain will come up later. We would all meet back aboard for CC and see everyone's "take" on Lisbon and Belém.

I on the other hand was obligated (it turned out to be a good obligation) to that lunch promised to the young lady from the "fado" restaurant the night before. We met at "Mariscos do Mar" on the waterfront in Cascais, the weather was delightful with lots of sunshine, and we sat outside on the patio. Rachel, that was her name, Rachel Guzmán, was pretty impressive to look at – good looking to the extreme, light blue jacket over a black sweater, black slacks; it all suggested a really nice build; and, oh, a rakish Portuguese beret on that beautiful head. Remember, I'm at lunch but still on duty; AT would not disapprove, at least initially, of the private lunch. I learned Amy would hear about it and plie me for information in her room later on board.

After a glass of Portuguese red wine for her and a cold Sagres beer for me she opened the conversation. "Michael, muito obrigada pela conversa! I'm glad you could take some time for me, and I hope it turns out to be mutual. Like I said, your reputation precedes you! I've got that LP and cassete as well of "Mistakes of Our Youth" by Chico Buarque and guess I could call you 'Arretado' from now on." She laughed and we chatted until the food arrived, garlic shrimp in my case, and Portuguese 'bacalhau' (the national dish of codfish) for Rachel. She offered to pay the check, but remembering AT guidelines, I thanked her and said we would "go Dutch." She knew all about my books on Brazil and the "Letters" to the New York Times. (Uh oh, I'm thinking of the amorous adventures.) But more important, I knew nothing about her and we spent most of that initial conversation with her doing the talking.

"Miguel, I wish we had more time; I would give you the royal tour of Cascais, at least the Cascais I remember. That's the main reason I'm on this trip, to see the places where I grew up and maybe secondarily compare them to the home of my ancestors in Spain. You see, I spent the first fifteen years of my life here in Portugal and studied until the end of what you call 'high school' right up the hill in the Nuns of the Sacred Heart School. I want you to know the whole story, so my age and dates don't matter. I was born in 1943 right here in Cascais; the family left Portugal in 1958 and moved to San Francisco in California. I went to USF with the Jesuits (like you at Georgetown), and have been doing free-lance journalism in the Bay Area ever since. I'm sort of representing Dad and Mom on this trip, since Mom is ailing with severe arthritis and Dad's doing double duty at work and at home. I've been on my own in all kinds of good and bad situations doing the news stories, so they had no qualms about me seeing Portugal and Spain on a "safe" AT ship! Ha!

"My parents moved in pretty sophisticated social circles once they landed here. I'm sure you are at least partially aware of their story and that of others. We are Sephardic Jews, long – time "conversos" living in Spain. Somehow or other my family escaped the Dominicans and their Inquisition aimed at people just like us, I think because our people way back became indispensable to the Crown and the Church hierarchy in Toledo. You may have heard of Samuel Ben ha – Levi; I'll fill you in later. By the way when we get there, I'll give you a special tour as well! And explain more."

"Rachel, this is indeed a pleasure, and I'm so happy to meet you, but I've got to give you a disclaimer right away: my studies of Spanish (and Portuguese) were as you know in the U.S. at Jesuit schools. We were not taught that much about the Jews in Spain other than the very general knowledge of Maimonides and Al -Andalus days, the Edict of Granada in 1492, the forced conversions ('Convert or Leave') but the worst, that even the most faithful 'conversos' were always under suspicion. And in Spanish Letters, I've always been aware of Fray Luís de León's connection to your people. Nossa! It was his great, great grandmother who was Jewish! And he did translate the 'Song of Songs' into Spanish, a 'mortal sin' I guess. Otherwise, I'm abysmally ignorant. But his 'Vida Retirada' is my favorite Spanish poem."

"Mike, I appreciate your candor and honesty. Maybe I can fill in some gaps for you, in Toledo for sure, but maybe even here in Portugal. I'll just leave it for now that in Spain in 1942 (for that matter, 1492) it was not good to be a Jew, even though a significant part of the national patrimony owes its existence to either confiscated Jewish wealth or their counseling of the wealthy Spaniards. Francisco Franco was way too enthusiastic about guaranteeing Spain's 'Catholic' tradition of Church and Family, including maintaining the church hierarchy, and more importantly 'flirting' with 'Der Füehrer' for any of my people to feel safe. Fortunately, we had the means and the contacts to get out of Toledo, transferring family assets by wire via banker friends, and reaching safety in Lisbon. You will currently hear scathing remarks about Portugal's long – time president and dictator Antônio de Salazar, especially since his death (difficult to defend yourself when you're dead) and the Revolution in 1974. But it was his basic belief in humanity that allowed him to follow a totally 'unofficial' diplomacy of allowing Jews from Eastern Europe to escape Hitler and his cronies and come to Portugal and then move on to other countries, mainly England and the United States. This was all happening just as what would become the Holocaust was taking serious form. Since the Guzmáns had those means, Dad and Mom got the visas. She was pregnant with me when they traveled at night and by automobile to the Spanish border, bribed the guards to pass, and twenty hours later reached safe haven with friends and relatives in Lisbon.

"You did not have to know all this, but as you Nebraska cowboys say, 'Put your cards on the table.' Are we still friends?"

"Rachel, we are not only friends but I shall take every opportunity to learn from you. Wow! This is great! I doubt our guides will talk much of your side of the story here. One thing – I've got to mind my p's and q's as an AT employee, be available to all the adventurers, but I can safely say that whenever possible I'll make time for you. And I'm sure there will be time on excursions and at some meals to get to know each other better."

Rachel smiled, a stunning smile, nodded her head and said, "You've already made my trip a success. I hear you brought your guitar on board, so I'll look forward to singing along on some of those Chico Buarque songs."

I said, "That won't take long, I only know a couple. Remember: 'Gringos can't dance samba.' But I know a lot of U.S. folk songs, good ole' country classics and can play some classical guitar pieces. Have you met Eli our music guy? HE'S the one that can pull it all together."

We chatted for about an hour on what we all had seen that morning, and promised to see each other on board. I explained I had to get back to the ship and prepare a short introduction to our trip tomorrow to Sintra. Rachel said, "I grew up going to Sintra on weekends and have hiked that trail up to the Moorish castle I'll bet half a dozen times. You've got a treat in store tomorrow. See you at CC."

As planned, I took the "elétrico" back to the "Cais de Sodré," a taxi to the ship and holed myself up in the room preparing notes for an Introduction to Sintra which would come at the end of our first CC that afternoon.

CC AND HARRY DOWNING

Harry Downing our glorious leader took the floor, welcomed all to our first CC in Portugal, said he hoped all were pleased so far, thanked me for the introduction to Lisbon and commented that our guides were unusually helpful. He went on to explain the plan for the next two days, still with on – shore excursions before reboarding IA for the next main port of O Porto. There would be a full day in Sintra with its not one but three major castles, its shops famous for Portuguese "louça" or ceramic tableware and lodging tomorrow night in a fine hotel in Sintra. The next day would be a coach trip to the seaside resort of Nazaré, a short visit to the major medieval Cistercian Monastery of Alcobaça on the way, and with options to Fatima and Leiria in the p.m. before the return to Lisbon and IA.

Harry then squeezed in one of his favorite topics – the political alliance between Portugal and English back in 1386 and an important link to it in the hills beyond Sintra. Tomorrow we would see the same thing General Wellington saw from the parapet of the Sintra Castle - Napoleon's troops bivouacked in the hills beyond Sintra. Wellington was instrumental years later, and again in 1814 in the ensuing major battle of the peninsula in retaking Portugal and Spain from Napoleon, restoring its crown to the Braganças who shortly returned home from exile, of sorts, in Brazil in 1814. Harry said in his King's English, "You know, it's a fascinating story, one we should all appreciate. The founder of Portugal, Prince Affonso Henriques of Bergundy, enlisted the help of English crusaders to drive the Moors from Portugal and became its first King. That same alliance is alive today and was instrumental in the war against Napoleon from 1809 to 1814 culminating in Waterloo. The conflicts in Spain and Portugal after the defeat of Napoleon - the liberal – conservative battles and unrest really aided in the huge move of Independence of Spain's colonies in America and Portugal's Brazil."

Brazilian diplomat Leonel Peixoto was invited by Harry to fill in the blanks regarding the Portuguese Royal Family, their escape to Brazil in

1808 and only returning with Napoleon's defeat in 1814. The famous "Eu fico" ["I'm staying"] speech of their son Pedro astounded the Portuguese royalty and the world – he stayed in Brazil and was instrumental in the Constitutional Monarchy which would last until 1888! His son Pedro II was one of the greatest and most enlightened rulers in all Brazil's history.

I thoroughly enjoyed it all, quaffing a couple of cold beers at the lounge bar, saying hello to Rachel and others, spending some time with Amy who said she thought we should have a talk later that evening. Dinner would come first with a wonderful conversation, my first, with Father David Siqueiros, a Jesuit priest from Goa, India. Dinner.

But before dinner I was given 15 minutes to introduce adventurers to the history and importance of Sintra. Here's the short historical overview. The Moorish fort may have existed since the 8th or 9th century A.D. Earliest times show it as a Moorish establishment with fort, this as early as the 11th century. The ubiquitous Affonso Henriques captured Sintra in 1147 from the Moors after the fall of Lisbon. One story has it that Christopher Columbus, now sailing for the Spanish Crown, was blown off course in 1493, spotted the rock of Sintra and sailed safely into Lisbon harbor.

The architect of Batalha Church, Boitac, built the Hieronymite monastery of Nossa Senhora da Pena in 1507. The building would evolve into the "Palácio da Pena." It would become the summer palace of the Portuguese royal family the Braganças in the 18th and 19th centuries.

I concluded by just giving a summary of the places we would experience the next day. I'll leave details for the actual time in that incredible place. Three castles! A town that looks like Fantasy Land in Disney Land! And important links to Napoleon, the Duke of Wellington and poets!

Later that evening there was cause for my head to spin – the dinner with Father David Siqueiros of the Society of Jesus from the city of Goa in India. He was I'm guessing in his late thirties, a young and very handsome priest. We shared a bottle of "vinho verde" and enjoyed dinner. My part of the conversation was mainly questions; I was abysmally informed of the long, rich and controversial history of the Jesuits in India. I knew Jesuit

Father Francisco Xavier was among the first to go there and that the Portuguese Crown approved of the Jesuits leading the expansion of the faith and evangelization. But no more. I found out later that India and Goa was the third most important Jesuit sites after Portugal and Spain!

Before I go on, the basic question was why was a Jesuit priest on the "International Adventurer?" Father David explained, a bit embarrassedly, "Professor Michael, it all is a gift. One of our order's benefactors in Goa, one of my own students now influential in the national government and grateful for the intellectual formation we gave him in our 'colégio' in Goa said, 'You need a vacation, a change of pace from those dusty halls of academia, and I'd like you to see your religious 'roots' in comfort!' Michael, if I may call you that, I said that would be preferable to the standard Jesuit visit to friends, schools and such with the constant need to 'be a Jesuit.' This way, in civilian clothes, I can enjoy life a bit more and maybe garner a perspective I wouldn't have otherwise."

Little did he know.

You take adventurers on their terms, you do your job, you try to be helpful, and make sure they enjoy themselves and accomplish their goals for the trip. So I tried to not ask too many questions. David (we dropped the 'Father' from that moment on at the dinner) was curious to know about my own education at Creighton and Georgetown and how in the world a farm boy from Nebraska became a publishing scholar on Brazil! He had traveled in Brazil and visited several fellow Jesuits in the post Vatican II era, even visited the new settlements and schools of the Liberation Theology generation. And not without danger; he was advised before he left Goa to travel as an "interested tourist."

I told him of the "cordel" and its deep historic roots to Catholicism, Jesus, Joseph, Mary and the Saints, and a mischievous Satan, promising to say more in a talk on board down the way. We agreed to do it again, dinner that is, and in turn he said he would fill me in more on the Portuguese in India. I said that hopefully when we got to Spain there would be some kind of an on – shore excursion to Loyola in Basque Country; that really got his attention.

The evening was topped on with a visit to Amy's room. She was tired and a bit irritable – dealing with on shore excursions day after day was a lot more difficult than the trips at sea when there were many days with no such demands. We sat together, had a drink of her good scotch, maybe spooned a bit (the reader may get tired of this old term from my parents' days, but I like it and it says it all; if you don't get it, get out Webster's Dictionary). We both agreed the trip was going smoothly for the most part with good things to come. Uh, she did ask me about that lunch and Rachel again.

5

SINTRA

ADVENTURERS' EXCURSION TO SINTRA

This is a Michelin Three Star Attraction and it lived up to that rating. The adventurers were up at 7:30, a hearty breakfast on board, and vans to Rossio Station at 9:00. The train to Sintra left at 9:08! We all felt like commuters. As we left, the station was jammed with many trains and all the commuter traffic. The scenery to Sintra was null and void until we reached the outskirts of Sintra on a trip of 18 miles and in 45 minutes by the "comboio," the strange name Portugal has for such trains.

All of a sudden there is a huge castle high on a hill to the left. Spectacular! There are three palaces in town: the 16th century Royal Palace in the town center, the Moorish Castle on the hill and the Bragança palace the "Palácio da Pena" way up on the mountain, the most recent.

We went to the palace in town first. The royal palace in the town center is the best-preserved medieval palace in Portugal, lived in continuously from the 15th to the late 19th century. After two hundred years the place was really added to and remodeled by King Manuel. The result is that one half of the Royal Palace is Manuelino Style, and there is more recent architecture in the other. The inside was full of the famous blue Portuguese tiles ["azulejos"] but made for Manuel in Sevilla in Spain. The guide noted that furnishings were Spanish, Moroccan, East Indian, and Brazilian. It reminded a bit of the Gulbenkian and John Paul Getty grounds and museum near Los Angeles. The tour included the huge bakery with its large chimney. One room with its painted ceiling had a theme of "magpies," another with swans ["cisnes"], a painting of the twenty-seven-year-old daughter of King Dom Diniz and Spanish wife Isabella, the Coat of Arms of the Avis Dynasty and its descendants, and the tale of a prince held prisoner (he was "louco") for nine years. Shades of Prince Segismundo in the Spaniard Golden Age Playwright Calderón de la Barca's famous "La Vida Es Sueño"! The Bragança nobility, in particular Queen Amélia, liked the place and still used it as a part time residence in the 19th century. It became a national monument in 1940. The kitchen was a castle in itself; they must have eater well.

The town center seemed like "Fantasyland" in Disneyland in Los Angeles, perhaps with good reason – Disney did research and copied palaces and castles at his place of business. The Spaniards, however, say the big palace in Segovia is the model for the castle of "Fantasyland." There were palaces with turrets and parapets all about. We would have time there late afternoon and evening.

THE PALÁCIO DA PENA

Palácio da Pena, Sintra

Adventurers took AT vans up the steep hill to the "Palácio da Pena" or "Cliff Palace." It is considered one of the major sites of 19th Century Romanticism in the world! I believe it; the heart not the mind inspired this place! They describe it as Neo-Gothic, Neo-Manueline, Neo-Islamic and Neo-Renaissance. A hodge – podge. It's all there. It became a summer residence for the Braganças and is still used on special occasions by the head of state of Portugal. Not to be missed! It dates to the 14th century but it was King Manuel I (Avis) who ordered a monastery built on the site with, who else, the "Jerônimos" in charge. The earthquake of 1755 reduced most of it to ruins but King Ferdinand and Queen Maria II had it rebuilt in the mid-19th century. Several different architects of different nationalities participated. One note is that one of them specialized in castles along the Rhine and brought a splash of those fairy tale castles to "Pena."

One might recall from earlier comments by diplomat Leonel Peixoto that the same royal family the Braganças fled to Rio de Janeiro during Napoleon's invasion of Portugal around 1803 and only returned in

1814 – minus son Pedro who would become Emperor of Brazil with his "I'm staying" ["Eu fico"] speech from the "Palácio do Paço" in "Praça 15" in Rio de Janeiro. The palace in one sense was almost a bit humorous – such a mess of styles! It appeared to be the result of a drunken party by a half dozen architects gathered together to outdo each other!

General Wellington's View, Palácio da Pena, Sintra

One recalls all the blue tiles, stone lattice work, gargoyles of crocodiles, but most impressive were the high parapets with the view toward Lisbon and the Rio Tejo to one side, to Cascais to the west, and up north along the Atlantic Coast. It was said that the Duke of Wellington spied Napoleon's troops from the NW parapet and soon the battle to retake the peninsula ensued. This would be in 1808. I'm not sure if that is just "guide talk" or not.

It was a truly spectacular view. There was a fierce wind from the ocean side. Maybe a sign for Mike Gaherty to be careful of high places. My readers recall the "Castillo" in Chichén – Itzá from my last book on Mexico. One recalls the interior rooms with "gesso" or plaster decoration in the Arabic "mudéjar" style and also much marble and wood. There were many tapestries, Persian and the like, many chandeliers and candelabras. But it still seemed a bit old and dingy, a bit freaky. It was difficult to imagine the steep ride up the mountain by horse drawn carriage!

THE "CASTELO MOURO" FROM THE "PALÁCIO DA PENA"

The Castelo Mouro, Sintra

Whew! One more castle to go. There is an amazing history to the Moorish castle half – way down the hill to the center of Sintra: after the loss of Córdoba in Spain to the Moorish Almorávides dynasty in 1031, the King of Badajoz

50

opted to transfer to Alfonso VI of León and Castile some territories on the Iberian Peninsula, among them the castle at Sintra. Afonso Henriques in 1147 with the capture of Lisbon took control of this place as well.

From the parapets of the Palácio da Pena one actually looks DOWN on the "Castelo Mouro." One can imagine the Moorish defense of the area from the high parapets and what the Portuguese must have had to do to take the old Moorish Castle and then keep it from the Spaniards and later the French. I felt queasy walking the narrow walkway along its wall. I wasn't the only one. An adventurer leaning too far over one of the old fort walls (in this case fortunately just four or five feet to a shelf before a huge drop – off) fell, badly scraped his arms and legs and was badly bruised. An ambulance arrived shortly and transferred him to emergency care in Sintra. He would be all right and continued on the trip. For old timers, it was Wonky of past fame on AT trips to Brazil and Mexico.

From the Moorish Castle there are views up to the "Palácio da Pena" and down to the main plaza in town. Most of us decided to walk down; it was a long, long hike down the trail but through great forest! (This was the hike Rachel Guzmán had talked about in Cascais.) The latter was carefully planned and has trees from throughout the world.

"LOUÇA" AND SHOPS

There was time for sightseeing in the main plaza where we saw the outstanding examples of Portuguese ceramic pottery. In retrospect, the ole' professor admits he was scared to death of the heights and edging around the parapets of the "Palácio da Pena" and then the walls of the Moorish castle. But this is what Portugal and Spain are all about! I never saw a castle wall or walkway that I did not want to climb! I will speak much of this later, including the cliché of "castles in Spain," but suffice to say Portugal indeed has its share, and in one sense is just a "small Spain."

That night there was a delightful stay at a beautiful inn and fine Portuguese cuisine and wines. It was there I met yet another of our amazing adventurers with ties to Portugal – Maurício Salazar, a great nephew of the deceased famous Antônio Salazar. The conversation was pretty one – sided, me listening, he talking. He was a bit veiled in his comments on Portuguese politics, understandable taking into account the 1974 Revolution just three years ago. But he said he had visited Brazil many times, mainly to Rio and Bahia, had read my "Adventures of a 'Gringo' Researcher in Brazil in the 1960s" which was pre – trip suggested reading on my bio page for this trip by AT, and said we had to talk about the "cordel." His father was a lawyer with the requisite degree from Coimbra and a bibliophile, and the "literatura dos cegos" ["blind men's' literature"] the Portuguese antecedent to the "literature de cordel" had caught his attention. We agreed to talk later when there was a "calm" in activities.

A BELATED CULTURAL NOTE ON SINTRA:

Portugal's classic dramatist Gil Vicente, its epic poet Camões and England's Lord Byron have all sung Sintra's praise (the latter in "Childe Harold"). I can understand why; there is a lot to brag about: the Moorish castle dates from the 8th century and includes ruins of a Romanesque chapel. The big palace of the town center was built in the 14th century with wings added on by King Manuel in the 16th. The Palácio da Pena was rebuilt in the 19th century by Fernando II, a Bragança, but includes ruins of an old Manueline chapel and cloister from the 16th century with its Portuguese tiles and Carrera marble altar. Sintra was the summer residence of Portuguese royalty for six centuries. The Convention of Sintra in 1808 early in the Napoleonic war allowed the French trapped in Portugal to retreat. That was probably a big mistake. The Duke of Wellington came on, huge battles ensued throughout Portugal, Spain and Russia, and the finally treaty was in 1814 in Paris.

That night in my room I got a phone call from Amy; she was still on board the IA, extremely busy with shore excursions mainly for the O Porto area, said she missed me and maybe we could get together in two days when all would return to Lisbon, board the ship, and have a leisurely day at sea before O Porto. She wondered about the excursions and asked me if I had met anyone interesting. I mentioned Rachel, emphasizing the Sephardi connection and her parents' arrival in Cascais, but no more. At that point Amy was not particularly curious; that would come later when she saw her at CC on board and our brief conversation at the bar. Uh oh.

6

NAZARÉ AND ALCOBAÇA ALONG THE WAY

The main attraction that next day, depending on your point of view, would be one of the most beautiful of sea scenes in Portugal, the small, quaint tourist town of Nazaré, but maybe for some Alcobaça and its historic Cistercian Monastery along the way would be far more important. Both merit some time.

And even before Alcobaça the vans stopped at a memorable scene for those of us who had read Cervantes and "Don Quixote de la Mancha," Portugal's version of the windmills or "molinos de viento," ["moinhos de vento"] a major episode in the novel. We stopped, climbed up to them and took pictures and I had a chance to retell in short order the "Molino de Viento" episode of the "Quixote."

Monastery of Alcobaça

And then it was on to Alcobaça, one of the jewels of all time in Portugal. The monastery was founded by no less than Affonso Henriques in approximately 1153 to pay a promise to the Blessed Virgin for her help in his victory over the Moors at nearby Santarém marking one of the high points of the Portuguese "Reconquista." The plan was to consolidate the young king's authority in the area and promote colonization to the area. The ticket would be the Cistercians under Bernard of Clairvaux who would build a major medieval monastery. It was huge by any measure with a 350-foot-long nave, 70-foot-high Gothic vault, Gothic portal and windows. There were many additions in the 16th century. It is indeed one of the major monasteries of all Europe!

Our guide was all right and even graciously allowed "the American professor" to tell once again how Portuguese Literature enters our story – the background being dynastic love affairs. Famous in Portuguese History and Letters were King Pedro and his lover Inés de Castro, his Spanish lady-in-waiting. Their love affair told in a romantic legend known to all is still required reading in Portuguese grammar schools. Alcobaça Monastery held their tombs which are considered the best examples of sculpture of the 14th century in Portugal. Inês was disliked by Pedro's father Afonso IV who feared Castilian influence in Portugal; he ordered Inês's death by decapitation. Upon learning of this Pedro who truly loved her and claimed she was the lawful queen and inheritor had her killers murdered, their hearts ripped out "because they had none" and then according to legend commanded all in the Portuguese court to pay homage to her by kissing the rotting bones of the hand of the corpse! The sarcophagi in Alcobaça depict Pedro and Inês both rising to look at each other before entering eternity. The sides of the same sculpted tombs depict the hell reserved for their enemies.

Other highlights in the monastery were the huge cloister built and inspired by Dom Dinis in the 15th century, the dining hall and kitchen with a small stream channeled through, the sleeping quarters and finally the Room of the Kings, "Salão dos Réis." The latter had "azulejos" on all sides depicting the history of the founding of the Monastery, in particular Affonso Henriques on his knees praying for the intercession of the Virgin against the vile Moors at the Battle of Santarem.

Late that morning the vans took everyone to Nazaré, an incredibly beautiful seaside town facing the Atlantic. The town was beautiful, old, had narrow streets, whitewashed houses, lots of Portuguese blue tile, and laundry hanging from balconies, much like the old Alfama in Lisbon. It is a major tourist site for northern Europeans and the British during July and August. We were ahead of them in June.

The Beach of Nazaré

But there's much more to Nazaré than tourism. Aside from being a fisherman's town along the sea, the town is considered a national monument. Above the small, quality beach in a crescent with wonderful waves, the ocean a turquoise-blue in the sunshine, there are high cliffs to one side (the highest in Portugal along the Atlantic Coast) and a funicular up the mountain to the "Nossa Senhora do Nazaré" shrine and church. Vasco da Gama was here before and after the India trip! One can see why it is a favorite tourist spot for the English as well as others from Northern Europe, especially during the hot days of August when the tiny place is transformed. Now in early June we had it to ourselves; in August the entire beach is crammed with beach tents and umbrellas.

From the top of the cliffs there was a magnificent view of the town below and out to sea. On this hill is the church of "Nossa Senhora do Nazaré" which owes its existence to the legend of Dom Fuas Roupinho from 1182. Hunting with friends, he was in hot pursuit of a deer and arrived at the precipice overlooking the ocean in the midst of heavy fog.

Suddenly realizing he would go over the edge he appealed to the Virgin asking her aid; she responded and he and his horse were saved in midair. The chapel of the Virgin remains on the cliff edge. Of importance is the fact that the huge cult of the Virgem do Nazaré in Belém do Pará in Brazil is based upon the same Statue of the Virgin, but in a different setting. The feast days in Brazil last for an entire month!

One of the churches in town displayed exterior walls entirely of azulejos and beautiful images and flowers within. This church is linked to the Portuguese fishermen and families. They fished the outer banks, caught millions of cod and many immigrated to Portuguese New England in places like New Bedford, MA. There they are associated with the huge whaling industry; many of the residents migrated not from the mainland but from the Azores which were already involved with the harvesting of whales in the Atlantic.

The best word for the town is "quaint." The narrow streets of the town were of cobblestone, and, as mentioned, we saw laundry on the balconies of the white washed houses and there were flowers about. It was a truly pretty scene. My group from the ship had a large meal at the Ribamar Restaurant: "sopa de mar," a shrimp omelet, and "robalo" or sea bass. Then walking out to the beach, we saw this scene: the women, fishermen's wives, are picturesque; during the day they sit in the sand weaving clothing while wearing black shawls and a short skirt with many petticoats. The men are in plaid shirts with long black stocking caps. In the late afternoon, between about 5 and 7 p.m. the men are also lying on the beach talking, the women knitting. A few tourists are along the "passeio" gawking at this "folkloric" sight. (I think arranged by the local tourist bureau.) At least part of the daily catch was displayed on drying racks on the beach during the sunny part of the day. I asked and was told they were "carrapu," Portuguese Mackerel.

Old Time Fishing Boat

One of the last scenes on that beautiful day, along with the fish racks, the ladies knitting on the beach, and the men mending nets, was the felicitous moment of spying one of the old-style traditional fishing boats. Some tourists and locals mingled to enjoy it all.

A tourist aside: as mentioned, Portugal is a principal site for tourists from England and we met several of them in our journey to the north. We were in Nazaré well before high season, but in the European months of vacation of July and August the village is jammed with tourists. The weather is then much warmer and all love the beach. One tourist would tell us of the British tourist route: the ferry across the sea from England to the coast of France and the "freeway" directly down the coast to Spain and Santander and west toward Spain's Santiago de Compostela and then down to Portugal. It is to be noted that the principal market for Portugal's wines including its famous "Port" is indeed England.

Harry and Amy were keeping us busy and out of trouble. Vans would give us all a very short ride to the next stop, turning out to be one of my favorites in Portugal, the tiny, fortified town of Óbidos and an evening in its wonderful "pousada" (Portugal's version of the "paradores") in the old castle keep.

ÓBIDOS

Walled Town – Castle of Óbidos

The town is small and quaint, a medieval town within a wall. Inside the walled city is a castle at one end which today has been converted into a "Pousada" built into the wall. The original castle and wall were built by the Moors and had been used to fortify the coastal route. They were rebuilt by the Portuguese after the town was freed by Affonso Henriques in 1148. King Dom Dinis and his queen visited in 1228. She was taken with the place so he gave the town to her as a gift! The tradition of the Portuguese king giving the town to his queen continued until 1833. More incidental historical notes: in 1491 King João II (Avis dynasty) died in Santarém and his body was found in the "Rio Tejo." His wife Queen Leonor went to Óbidos to mourn. Much later The Duke of Wellington spied the French army from Óbidos in 1808 and thus began the first battle of the campaign to retake the peninsula. As mentioned, the ramparts of the walls of Óbidos date from Moorish occupation but were restored in the 12th, 13th, and 16th centuries. The Castle Keep is on the north, the setting of today's "Pousada."

We walked as much of the walls as possible with a wonderful view and a sense of history! Part of that is a church, St. Mary's of Óbidos. The inside walls of St. Mary's Church were entirely of "azulejos"! The guide said King Alfonso V married his eight-year-old cousin Isabella here in 1444. Hmm. The rest of the town is quaint with pretty stucco houses, many flowers, cobblestones, tile roofs and azulejos. It really is a small place, quite compact.

The night in the 'Pousada' at Óbidos. This was exciting for me – my first (and so far only) night in a real castle! They had space heaters in the rooms that did not quite do the job, and the water in the showers was only luke warm (I am wondering, is this the case or custom in all Portugal? Brrr! They get a pass.) Decorations were complete sets of medieval armor in the reception area, the main hallways and the dining room and huge colorful banners hanging from the ceilings. I thought I had arrived at the place of all my dreams! I sat with adventurers from London and we had the good fortune to have Harry Downing at our table. We were almost in tears with laughter with Harry telling English jokes, and jokes of Brits in Portugal, all while all of us downing (an appropriate play on words) perhaps a few too many glasses of rosé, "vinho verde," after dinner Port and even Madeira wines. I even had a chance to tell my two favorite Brazilian jokes making fun of the Portuguese (in Brazil the Portuguese have the same fame as the "polocks" in the U.S.) The Londoners told of harrowing times on that journey – drive from France, through Spain to Galicia and down to Portugal.

After dinner I had drinks in the bar with Rachel and Maurício Salazar in the bar, surrounded by full sized suits of armor and banners. It was an opportunity for Rachel to introduce herself to him and explain her background and connection to Portugal, and I might add, thank him for his uncle's welcome stance to Jewish refuge in Portugal. It led to a "lecture" of sorts by Maurício of all the good things his uncle had done for Portugal, mainly keeping the country out of World War II, of the tightrope he had to walk between the Allies, Spain, and Germany. All this is true.

When I asked him of his view of 1974 and the "Revolução dos Cravos," the tone changed, "Uma tragédia, uma verdadeira tragédia. Portugal perdeu os restos de sua grandeza de nossa maior época. Os socialistas 'reinam' hoje em dia, a economia é estragada e temos uma verdadeira onda de refugiados d'África. O Portugal de meu tio 'já era.'" ["A tragedy, a true tragedy. Portugal lost the remains of grandeur of our greatest epoch. The socialists 'reign' today, the economy is in shreds and we have a true inundation of refugees from Africa. The Portugal of my uncle is 'long gone.'"] Maurício was ten years older than Rachel or so I but I thought he might still be "hitting on" her; stranger things have happened. I did catch her glancing at me fairy often with what can I say, "provocative eyes." Hmm.

7

ON TO FÁTIMA AND BATALHA

The next day, our last of several of the foray out of Lisbon, we had two major places to see, the famous apparition site of the Blessed Virgin Mary at Fátima, and then yet another of the major historic sites for the foundation of Portugal and its battles and independence from Spain, the Monastery of Batalha. Then in late p.m. we would make our return to the IA in Lisbon, say our goodbyes to the same with the Captain's dinner and entertainment on the back deck, and then begin a very leisurely night and next morning "at sea" to O Porto.

FÁTIMA

I accompanied one of the vans with guide to Fatima, noting that Father David was along, but now in clerical blacks with white collar. The early morning visit to Fátima was short. Pleasure before business: we stopped at a "confeitaria had delicious hot "bicas" and from the bakery and a first, apropos of the occasion: huge slices of "pão de ló" or Angel Food Cake. Between the sugar in the coffee and the cake most of us were primed for the day.

On the 13th of each month, especially in May and October, huge crowds of pilgrims come to Fátima to remember the dates of the first and then the final apparitions of the Virgin Mary to the peasant children. On May 13,

1917, the Virgin appeared from an oak tree to three shepherds, Francisco, Jacinta and Lúcia, and her message was a call for peace (it is 1917 and World War I still rages) and the conversion of Russia. On October 13, 1917, seventy thousand people were present and saw the rain stop and the sun shine and begin to revolve in the sky like a ball of fire. The Bishop of Leiria authorized the belief in the apparitions in 1930.

We walked to the huge square of Fátima, impressive for its size and then to the modern chapel replacing the tiny original chapel. The new building has columns with statues which represent the place and figures of the original apparitions. There was a wonderful mass in English, the high point being the singing in Latin, including the "Pater Noster." It took me back to the days of my youth as an altar boy - "Introibo ad altare dei" - or something like that. I prayed for and offered the mass to my Mom, a life time devotee of Fátima. She said her Rosary religiously every night. I recall in the winter time her being wrapped in her robe in front of the small heat register in the dining room of the old farm house with her beads in her hands. She was a great believer in the messages of Fátima, particularly praying for the conversion of Russia!

I was very much moved by these brief moments in Fátima. As was Father David and many other adventurers. However, I heard one mutter, "Enough of this Catholicism; let's move on." I was attempted to ask him why in the hell was he on this trip to two of the most Catholic countries in the world; maybe it was the wine, seafood and angel food cake.

The Basilica itself is modern with stained glass windows depicting the apparition scenes. It houses the tombs of the three shepherds. They told us that just a few days earlier the huge plaza was jammed with pilgrims, numbering perhaps in the hundreds of thousands. It was practically empty when we visited that morning.

BATALHA – DIFFERENT BUT YET THE SAME

Our vans took us on to Batalha [The Battle] where we stopped for lunch at a busy working people's café. We saw a lady with eggs heading to the market and "pedreiros" [stone masons] working on a new sidewalk. Men in the café were talking of the 2-1 win by Benfica over Sporting in a soccer match. There had been large buses with flags waving zooming by heading home from Lisbon and the game.

I add a note from the travel diary as to the countryside we saw around Batalha. There were tiny plots of great variety – wheat, vegetables, many fruit orchards and mostly vineyards with what looked like a plentiful harvest of grapes on them. The roads were winding between the hills and were badly paved. The countryside seems densely populated. There were some "burros," a few oxen and many small garden tractors pulling small wagons also used as transportation on the country highways. The farmers do not appear poor, and there is a very Celtic-Irish look to many. Traffic was often clogged but there were no real traffic jams. As I write these notes I realize how small Portugal is but also how we really got a feeling for the countryside and the small towns north or Lisbon.

I was still simmering a bit from that exchange about "enough of this Catholicism" in Fatima, but soon forgot when we reached this very impressive place. I would recall it many times later in Spain, particularly at the Cathedral of Sevilla and in Toledo as well. Batalha merits an introduction. It might be the closest thing Portugal has to Chartres and even Cologne in Germany.

General Álvaro Nunes Pereira and Santa Maria da Batalha

This place marks a high point of Portuguese-Spanish history – the battle of Aljubarrota, 1385. Juan I of Castile, nephew of the deceased Portuguese king, and João I, Grand Master of the Order of Avis (crowned king in Portugal just seven days earlier) meet in battle to decide the crown of Portugal. João makes a promise to the Virgin to build a church in her honor should he win. He takes the day when his general Álvaro Nunes Pereira chases the Spanish all the way back to Castile. I do not think however the Virgin appeared in the clouds this time, but still, a promise is a promise. The result was the great Gothic church "Santa Maria da Vitória da Batalha." And Portugal becomes free of Spanish domination for two hundred years. This was the moment I was first introduced to Javier and Maria Madariga adventurers from New York but with long time ties to León in Spain. They said a bit too loudly outside that tremendous medieval Gothic portal, "Esto no es nada! You shall see - our day is coming soon. If Spain had won that battle, there would be no Portugal, just Spain from one end of the peninsula to the other. And by the way, speaking Portuguese is like speaking Spanish but with mush in your mouths. And Portugal would not be the back-water place it has been for the last 700 years!" I thought we would have our first fist fight right then. Anyway …

The real name of the sublime edifice is the "Mosteiro de Maria Vitoriosa da Batalha;" it was begun in 1388 by a Portuguese architect. Then construction continued in 1402 to 1438 by Houget, an Irish architect who did the "Founder's Chapel" in "flamboyant Gothic."

King João I (Avis), spouse Philippa of Lancaster and son Prince Henry the Navigator are buried here. I digress to tell of this famous son. It all started with the impetus of "Henrique o Navegador." He had encouraged his father to invade Ceuta in Northern Africa and also got everyone interested in the legend of Christian Prester John. Defeating the Moors in Ceuta also temporarily solved the problem of the Barbary pirates who had invaded the coast of Portugal and hauled off victims to the African slave market. It was Henry who was instrumental in the Portuguese development of the "Caravela" or light sailing ship that could tack into the wind; these were the ships that would soon conquer the sea lanes, to the east to India, to the west to Brazil. Henry was incidentally governor of the Order of Christ, the Portuguese version of the Knights of Templar in the city of Tomar. The Templar funds aided him in obtaining the goods and the ships to carry out his goals. His place of work was Sagres in the Algarve where he gathered map makers and navigators. It is said that the greatest secrets of the ages were indeed the maps! All led to the discovery of the Azores and to the famous later expeditions of Bartolomeu Dias (the Cape of Good Hope) and Vasco da Gama's epic journey to India. We have plans later to see Sagres! On a lesser note, adventurers noted that a major brand of beer in Portugal is indeed "Sagres."

The main cloister of Batalha Monastery was done by Portuguese architect F. D'Évora who also did the Alfonso V Cloister in Gothic style. However, successor architects like Boiytac used the Manueline style in the arches of the cloister and in the Octagonal Royal Chapel (it was to be King Duarte's tomb). All work was abandoned by King João III (1521-1557) who favored doing a NEW monastery by the Hieronymites in Belém, the same one we described in previous pages. The Dominicans would administrate old Batalha.

Some architectural tidbits of interest at the Batalha Monastery:

> The stained glass above the main altar is 16th century Manueline style.

> The Fleur-de-Lis balustrade on the entire cloister combines Gothic and Manueline. There are flowered pinnacles, and slender columns with decorations of coils, pearls and shells.

> The vaulting of the Chapel House is square, twenty by sixty feet, without supporting columns. The window is 16th century.

> One enters the unfinished chapels via a Gothic Porch with the doorway in Manueline style of 16th century.

> Added to the Octagonal Chapel is a Renaissance Balcony done by King João III in 1533.

> The important characteristic of the Gothic, the flying buttresses, support the main walls, allowing them to be thicker with larger vaults.

Most impressive and memorable for me may be the portal or main door of Batalha Monastery. The huge doorway is entirely carved in stone with Christ in Majesty in the center, the four evangelists in the tympanum, the twelve apostles to the side and angels, prophets, kings and saints in the arching. It is one of the famous stone carved Gothic doorways in Western Europe (thus my early remarks of Cathedrals in Sevilla and Toledo).

After spending most of the day seeing the ins and outs of the Monastery, we had a 3 p.m. "lanche" including "Vinho Verde" and a taste of "Porto" in an incredibly busy, middle-upper class "confeitaria" or tea room located in a shopping area in Batalha. There were ladies dressed in high heels and their Sunday best, children nicely dressed, men in coat and tie, all gulping down "bicas," huge pastries, "sandes" or dainty sandwiches, and drinks. It was a very polite Sunday afternoon outing! We sat back, relaxed and enjoyed it.

There were a couple of interesting moments at the tea house. Wonky was taking a picture from a parking spot in front of the tea shop and a dwarf stepped in to park a car behind him. A little boy saw pastries in the glass window of the "confeitaria" and licked the glass case in front.

After those exhausting three days of excursions our motorcoach took us all the way back to Lisbon, not really that long a drive. We went past the new University of Lisbon and one of the Portuguese on board said it was the greatest, up to date, and old Coimbra was just a relic. Our titular Portuguese Linguistics Professor from O Porto Antonio Saraiva busted him in the chops, defending both o Porto and Coimbra. We had to separate them, Antônio apologizing profusely, the "Lisboeta" chagrinned but finally they shook hands. I did not know professors could box so well.

Everyone seemed happy to be back aboard, to get cleaned up and ready for what would be a spectacular CC covering all that history and tourism. The Captain's Dinner would follow and then a half day of relaxation at sea before we docked in O Porto. Coimbra would follow.

It was great to be back "home" and to see Amy. There was one bit of interesting news: Chico Buarque was scheduled to give a one – night concert in Lisbon (I'm not sure how he wangled the DOPS permission from the military dictatorship in Brazil to leave the country). Always a big success in the mother country, he was now even more so due to his praise – panegyric "Tanto Mar" of the Revolution of the Flowers back in 1974. Amy and I talked to Captain Tony proposing an addition to our return to Lisbon on our way back down the coast from La Coruña and Santiago de Compostela in Spain; IA would dock for one night only and perhaps have a reprise of Chico's concert on board in Brazil back in 1973. Tony remembered the big success in Brazil and knowing Chico had many fans aboard, was open to it all. Amy, ever the "go – getter" had already made contact with Chico's agent in Lisbon proposing the idea. Cables were going back and forth to Chico in Brazil and we were assured the agent would get us on the ship via ship – to – shore line in O Porto with news. Chico and Marieta had loved the night on the "International Adventurer" from Rio to Parati back in 1973. We might even be able to get them to stay on to Lagos in the Algarve.

CC THAT NIGHT

CC that night was a bit dicey with unexpected comments to some of the staff and adventurers' "take" on the past few days. The subject of Belém brought up the first tiff and Batalha the second. The issues were Vasco da Gama and the voyage to India followed by criticism of Portuguese plundering of Africa and India. That was brought up by a traveler from New Delhi I had not met, Mr. Singh. (I wondered why he was on the trip and would only find out days later. He turned out to be an industrialist from Delhi and a part owner of the line, on board to see what the Mother Country was like today.) Maurício Salazar testily answered him defending Portugal and its maritime and explorers' history. Father David usually very reticent about all this chimed in with the amazing things the Portuguese Jesuits had done in India.

The second controversy was the question of divine intervention in Portuguese and Spanish history, an altogether common occurrence according to old accounts – the "miraculous" role of the Virgin Mary at Santarém and the victory over the Moors in 1184 and at Aljubarrota in 1385 and the Spaniards with their own story of the Virgin Mary's incentives to Apostle St. James on his white horse leading the Spaniards to victory over the Moors in the same times. Harry Downing concluded in a bit of a sarcastic aside that if it weren't for the Virgin Mary, there certainly would be less tourism in Portugal – Alcobaça and Batalha and even Lisbon, not to speak of Nazaré and Dom Fuas and the deer! And he added, "At least we had the angels' intervention with the 'pão de ló' cake at Fátima" and laughed.

You learn to not argue about politics or religion most times, but we were in the wrong place to contest national history or religious beliefs or legend and myth. That is, IA staff and crew; Harry spoke to me in an aside, "We've never had such a volatile mixture of passengers on board. Keep an eye out and put on your black and white striped referee's shirt and hat.! Ha ha. We soon will be in another historic city, Portugal's second, and then its major medieval university town." We would travel 195 miles, IA's top speed 23 mph, but leisurely. Arrive late p.m. view of entrance to the Port.

THE CAPTAIN'S DINNER

Shortly after we all sat down and the first wine was served, Captain Tony took the floor, introduced long time IA chef, Reyaldo Romano and his staff, all in dress whites. We applauded and he said (I love the Portuguese saying) "A noite está só começando" ["the night is just beginning") so enjoy! It was seafood at its best, not all necessarily familiar to or favorites of the farm boy from Nebraska. A "mariscos do mar" soup to start us off (with some shelled critters I could not open), then a small broiled lobster (which I mangled but finally pried open), then three choices - large 'gambas' or shrimp stuffed with crab, 'róbalo' or sea bass, or the national dish –'bacalhau ao alho' [codfish in garlic sauce]. Fresh salads, two different kinds of rice, and yes, 'favas,' Portuguese beans! IA supplied the wine varying from red to white, light champagne to 'vinho verde,' and either Port or Madeira after dinner. No less than four Portuguese desserts followed: Pastel de nata (specialty from Belém), 'queijadas' (from Sintra,') 'flan,' and 'pão de deus,' the latter a sweet golden bread filled with cocoanut and my favorite.

Amy and I sat once again with my favorites, Leonel and Uíara Peixoto from Brazil, and we did a lot of comparing of Brazil and Portugal and the languages [o' Pa'] and after two or three glasses of wine they all insisted

I retell my Portuguese jokes from one of the talks! I loved them because I could do my imitation of continental Portuguese. "Cãáã! O' Pa.'" It is fair to say that there were two Portuguese at the table, Maurício Salazar and Antônio Saraiva nicknamed by staff as "the pugilist." As mentioned, he was a professor of linguistics from the University of O Porto; we would have great conversations with the next two days. I asked him if he might see if he could be in my group; Amy could easily arrange that. Maurício was still a little hot under the collar from the discussion (is that the right word?) about Portugal in India and the Far East, but soon warmed to the conversation and even gave his imitation of Brazilian accents and stereotypes- the "sleepy, lazy Bahianos" and the "cool Cariocas" and "all business Paulistanos." And not bad. He should have been the linguist. Leonel Peixoto had done a turn or two in Portugal, knew it well, so he was particularly equipped with anecdotes of the "portugas." They all wanted to know the language stereotypes for regions in the United States, but probably could imitate us better then we could ourselves! It's a bit of a difference in cultures, we don't dwell on such things as they do.

Amy and I had a reunion later that night in her room, both in a very good frame of mind after the dinner libations. Right away she said she wanted to be with me in O Porto and Coimbra. She had shore excursions all settled and said she would have the day at sea later to work again. I told her I was really sorry she was shackled to her desk on IA while we were having the great outings, saying I would have loved to be alongside her on the castle parapets in Sintra, the beach in Nazaré and that romantic pousada in Óbidos! "Hey 'arretado,' it's my job; I hear you are doing yours well, so me too!"

She had noticed Rachel Guzmán at C and C, and … uh … woman's intuition? She guessed that Rachel and I might click. I said it was all business, no more, no less. (I was wondering if adventurer "spies" had seen me with Rachel and Maurício in the bar in Óbidos?) But that I would welcome her help in Toledo in Spain. Amy lamented we had had, so far, little time together and wondered "where we stand." What to say?

"Nothing has changed; let's enjoy the trip and go from there." Kisses and hugs evolved into an intimate time, the first (and not last) on the trip. The good chemistry was confirmed. I would be giving a short introduction to O Porto tomorrow morning after Harry would fill us in on the importance of O Porto and the English − Portuguese Alliance. Once again, my first time in Porto and I would rely on Harry, Antônio Saraiva, and the local guides on − shore. Amy had been there before on IA and said there was a lot to see and experience and she hoped to share it with me.

8

O PORTO AND VILA NOVA DE GAIA

It was exhilarating to be back at sea, seemed a long time since Madeira to Lisbon. We were on our way to O Porto and Vila Nova de Gaia. 195 miles, IA's top speed 23 mph, but leisurely. We would arrive late around noon with a view of entrance to the Port.

I was up early, enjoyed the good coffee, fruit and pastries in my room still making notes for the introduction to O Porto later that morning. It was all interrupted by a call to the bridge – major whale sighting! Jack had spotted a pod of hunchbacks and we took thirty minutes to watch them spout, come up and even breach! All the naturalists and nature lovers on board loved it; the rest of us were in a bit of awe. It didn't leave much time before the two talks, Harry's major talk on England and Portugal and my short fifteen minutes introduction to O Porto before IA docked.

I won't go into detail but can only say Harry was informative, entertaining and even hilarious, up to snuff and expectations. You could tell we were now "on his turf," and he reveling in the moment (although he had probably given the talk at least fifty times before). How does one do seven centuries of history culminating in today's politics and tourism in 60 minutes? Of course, he digressed to tell of Henry the VIII, Ann Boleyn and the other wives, the Tudors, Queen Victoria and the German connection, and on down to Queen Elizabeth, the name change to the Windsors once more, and the alliance during World War II and the connection to Portugal. Unique in all Europe with its neutrality, Lisbon became a hotbed of espionage by both the Allies and the Axis, the two sometimes "neighbors" in Rossio Square and in Estoril where refugees ranged from European nobility to Jewish people desperate to get out of Germany and Eastern Europe and to somehow get to Brazil, England or the United States. Nobility from Hungary, Barcelona, Italy and Romania all made Estoril their homes during and after the War. Harry had to end with another of England's exports – the James Bond films and the scenes in the Estoril Casino in the first version. He quipped, "I think we have a bevy of Bond girls or look a likes on board even as I speak – you know who you are! Well, perhaps I should say 'retired' Bond girls." Much laughter ensued.

MIKE'S INTRODUCTION TO O PORTO

"Now that was as they say a 'hard act to follow.' It's a bit sketchy but here's O Porto. The notes are a little more academic since I know it only from studies. Harry will lead the way along with our usual guides. O Porto's historic center is fairly small, but the metro area is up to about one and one – half million. It is located on the estuary of the Douro River running from NE to SW, its main claim to fame with the Douro Grape and Wine country producing, you guessed it, Port Wine. More on that later. O Porto was originally an outpost of the Roman Empire that gave it is first name: Portus Cale. On the south banks of the Douro is really a district, but another city, Vila Nova de Gaia, and it is the main area of the famous flat-bottomed sailing boats – the "barcos rabelos" - which hauled huge casks of wine into O Porto on the Douro.

"O Porto originally was important as a post for the commerce between Lisboa and Braga in the north. The Moors had taken the area but a coalition of forces from Asturias, León and Galicia sent General Peves to reconquer it; he did succeed in 868.

"Porto's next important moment was the marriage of João I of Portugal and Phillipa of Lancaster in 1386 and the resulting oldest military alliance in Europe (the Treaty of Windsor). The alliance exists yet today.

"In the 14th and 15 century O Porto became known for its shipyards which built most of the sailing vessels which would mark the age of discovery to the Far East and to Brazil in the west. We will get a special personally guided tour of the same by our own proud Captain Tony who I am sure will not let us forget that 'International Adventurer' was built in the same yards.

"1415 is a major date in Portuguese History. Prince Henry (later Henry the Navigator) would lead a flotilla of ships and troops to northern Morocco to conquer the Moslems in Ceuta, starting out from O Porto, then Lagos. That would truly open the doors to exploration of the west coast of Africa and eventually to Vasco da Gama's trip in 1497 to India.

"We jump all the way to the 19th century when French troops take the city and are driven out in the same year by the Duke of Wellington, this in 1809, in what turned out to be just the first foray in the long Peninsular War. After the defeat of Napoleon, Portugal, like Spain, was thrown into decades of squabble and unrest from liberal – conservative conflicts. It all settled down only with the "Estado Novo" of Salazar from the 1920s to the 1970s.

"So it is not surprising that O Porto has at least eight major monuments worth seeing. One can see the rivalry with Lisbon! In our two days (plus one – half) we'll try to get to most of them:

For the religious and church architecture aficionados:

The Baroque Church called the "Torre de Clérigos" from 1732
The O Porto Cathedral, Romanesque
The Igreja do Carmo with its azulejos
Thc Episcopal Palace
And the largest Synagogue in the Iberian Peninsula. The Kadoorie Synagogue from 1938.

(There were several Jewish people on board, meeting them later. Rachel often sat with them at meals and called me over one time. The goy mainly listened, that is until we started talking of Jewish comedians. I told of the snippets of the great Cid Caesar Show we had seen back in Nebraska on black and white TV, but mainly of all the Mel Brooks movies I had seen. What I did not know or could not relate was the entire "dark side" of Jewish pogroms throughout history or even other than general details of the Holocaust. They were nice to me, perhaps because Rachel had told them of our lunch in Cascais.)

For the Secular minded, no less important are two major edifices:

The Stock Exchange

São Bento Train Station with its outstanding "azulejos."

"And for you sweet tooth fans, there is also a restaurant along the line of A Brazileira in Lisbon (and the "Confeitaria Colombo" in Rio). More stained glass, "bicas" and wonderful Portuguese pastries. … And of course, wine tasting at Vila Nova de Gaia.

"Are you exhausted yet? There is an extremely important one – day excursion out of O Porto later to Portugal's most famous university and medieval town Coimbra.

There was applause and Antônio Saraiva quipped, "O Brazileiro, or should I say, 'O Arretado' did well. You will learn there is quite a rivalry between Lisbon and we of O Porto. And for good reason!"

AFTERNOON AND NEXT DAY IN O PORTO

Since I was the "rookie," we depended on the guides who turned out to be quite good and Antônio Saraiva. Here are short vignettes of what we saw. First the historic district of old O Porto, from crowded commercial streets down by the river up to the tall towers of old monuments above. For maybe "ideological" reasons, that afternoon there was an option of walking the town and shopping or the Churches. Most came along for the churches when told there would be plenty of time tomorrow for the shopping and browsing.

The "Torre dos Clérigos"

The tower from 1732 and the façade most interested us. Six interior floors and over 200 steps. It was inspired by the "campaniles" of Italy as was the pediment of the Baroque façade, no wonder, the architect was from Italy. He also did the ...

Archbishop's Palace

Originally from the 14th century it passed through many stages and tribulations; but what we see today is the 18th century version in Portuguese Baroque with central doorway and three rows of windows. More spectacular is the interior stairway and Baroque portal on the second floor. The bishop fled in 1832 with internal Portuguese strife, and the building for a long time then became the seat of the municipality of O Porto.

The Cathedral (Igreja da Sé). O Porto

It dates back once again to the 1147 after O Porto was liberated from the Moslems. The old Romanesque church disappeared and, in its place, there are two square towers, a beautiful Gothic Rose window, but according to António, a royal mess and mistake when the original Romanesque portal was replaced with one in the Baroque style with columns, totally out of place with its origin and spirit. The interior reminds of Alcobaça a bit, but the gold gilt altar is definitely from the Baroque era. The two flying buttresses however remain, a vestige of what used to be. A Gothic cloister (a bit like Batalha) with wonderful azulejo scenes is impressive. The façade of the Cathedral reminded me a bit of the "Sé" in Lisbon, and of course originally was contemporary to it.

There are other beautiful churches in O Porto, many in fact; but the azulejo covered Igreja do Carmo was impressive. The azulejos were not added until the 20th century and were actually made in Vila Nova de Gaia. We recall the same at Alcobaça, Batalha and of course the Museum in Lisbon.

Dinner that evening was at the "A Brasileira" Café; those of us on IA in Brazil could only recall a "Confeitaria Colombo" in Rio and A Brazileira in Lisbon. I sat with Amy and Harry and Antônio Saraiva. I admitted that indeed O Porto had things rivaling and even surpassing Lisbon, the azulejos in particular. Antônio told of his academic visits to Brazil and a big conference on Camões and "The Lusiads" at the Portuguese Royal Reading Room" in Rio, a bit of a bore, but he got away to Copacabana a time or two.

Mike and Amy back on board. News from Rio and Lisbon: Chico Buarque agrees to a short visit on board. Here's the tentative plan: dinner with Chef Amato and short concert. The time will be in the evening in our one – night stay in Lisbon after we conclude all things north. Tomorrow is day 2, O Porto, next is day 3 – Coimbra – days 4 to 7 at sea to the north around the "corner" of Portugal to La Coruña in Galicia and Santiago de Compostela. Whew! After that two days at sea back down to Lisbon for Chico and Marieta. We dock, have dinner with Chico Buarque and Marieta. Then a funky short "show"; "Memories of our Youth" with Mike, old "samba" and "Tanto Mar."

DAY TWO IN O PORTO

A.M. Here's a preview of our plan: the two secular places - the Stock Exchange and the São Bento Train Station.

Lunch and wine at winery in Vila Nova de Gaia.

Nature Reserve of Douro Estuary for the naturalists. Later on board and CC.

P.M. Tour of the Shipyards with Captain Tony

Dinner back on board; what else? Wine tasting. Eli does O Porto Music with local 'fadistas'

How it all turned out that day.

In the a.m. we did those two secular points which were important: The Stock Exchange and the São Bento Train Station.

The Stock Exchange has one of the most beautiful rooms in O Porto. The Arab Room in the Moorish Revival Style is overwhelming in its beauty.

Just as impressive or more is the main room of the São Bento Train Station, the azulejo and polychromatic tiles overwhelmed our adventurers. You would think you would tire of such things, but when you compare to others in Portugal this shows the good sense the O Porto people had in maintaining the national heritage. Once again Prince Affonso (and King) is shown in the battle of Septa. But it is just one of many – the tiles depict Portuguese history in their own medium as much as Diego Rivera's "frescos" in Mexico City. Wow! We all were wondering "how can you top this?" Maybe you can't, but great things would await us the next day in Coimbra.

Lunch was in Vila Nova de Gaia after the winery tour. I think most adventurers needed to sit and and rest a while. Two adventurers get inebriated, almost fell off the "barco de rabelo" or wine boat, all this after lunch. There's not much to report except the quaint flat boats that used to come down the Douro with the barrels of wine, then the processing and aging in Vila Nova and then off to foreign parts, especially England.

The naturalists took a a good sized contingent out to the Nature Reserve of Douro Estuary, really their first chance at possibilities since the forest in Sintra. And it was a good day with about 40 sightings; we will get a report at CC.

P.M. Shipyards.

The final afternoon in O Porto belonged to Captain Tony and exec Martim when we got that promised tour of the shipyards where IA was built. He would fill all of us in at CC that night as well. It was all overwhelming, and I don't have the technical vocabulary to do it justice. Just imagine berth after berth with a total of perhaps a dozen ships at various points of production. Huge "guindastes" or cranes everywhere lifting steel beams to the superstructures. Hundreds of dock workers and construction workers in white overalls and protective helmets, like ants on an anthill if you saw from above. Captain Tony plied us with more statistics than I can remember or handle, the number of ships completed each year, the tonnage, the future owners and destinations. Details on "Adventurer" itself remained for a future talk at sea. Someone said, "Nossa, it's like going to a ship baby hospital." Guffaws.

CC that evening featured photos from the ecstatic naturalists, more than 40 species, and many that should not have been there, but mostly North Atlantic seabirds. Willie then took over with images of dives along the coast of Portugal and some spectacular whale pictures – and close up!

Dinner was pleasant, the food fine, the conversation jolly. I tried to move around a bit and converse with old and new adventurers. Rachel and friends were beaming after the Synagogue Visit and marveling that such a magnificent modern structure had come to be in O Porto, another example of positive politics toward Jewish emigrants from WW II and later years.

Someone suggested a wine drinking contest up in the lounge after dinner. What's this? The Portuguese were familiar enough with it (and a few of the Spanish crowd on board). It turned out to be a little like their version of poker: (you slug your small cordial glass of wine and "call" the opponent to do the same) the contestants on each side of the table, small cordial "after dinner" size glasses each filled with a variety of "aperitivo," dinner and then after dinner "fortified" wines. One progresses from the "light" to the not – so – light samples. It was agreed that after each glass the contestant would have to name a successive king from Portugal's many dynasties. (Harry scoffed, "Easy, easy, come to England if you want a real challenge, but I like the idea. It might ruffle those stuff – shirts at Oxford and perhaps we would get to see how they might be with their hair – I mean wigs - down!") Who else but Maurício Salazar and Antônio Saraiva were the contestants. After the Avis dynasty, they both agreed "to hell with it" and switched to each having to tell a Portuguese joke. That was when the fun started, granted, just for the Portuguese speakers, but many adventurers stuck around just to hear the two of them go at it. A draw was declared by Barman Dimitri when someone knocked over the entire table with cordial glasses flying everywhere. No broken glass due to the thick carpet, but alas, the Thai maids called to quickly clean up the wine stains. One of the Spaniards who accompanied it all said, "Gente, we'll do the same thing at Málaga, but it won't be this sissy wine – how about real Spanish coñac?"

AT trips are not normally along this line, but we got everyone to bed, announcing once again tomorrow would be an early day and off to Coimbra! Our two contestants – agreeing it was a draw due to the overturned table – were nursing severe hangovers. One said "bicas" were the only cure; the other said "yogurt." The other remarked, "I'd rather suffer the hangover."

9

COIMBRA IT IS

Our vans got on a "superhighway" - the "Expresso" - to Coimbra, so we made good time. There was heavy pine forest much of the way and nice, occasional brick and tile country homes with pretty flower gardens in front as well as many vegetable gardens. Here's what our guide told us when she met us in the main old town center plaza:

"Coimbra served as the capital of Portugal in the Middle Age, but is best known for the university, the oldest in the Portuguese speaking world. This small city (third largest in population in Portugal but important beyond its size) has all the pre-requisites: Roman, Visigoth, Arab and finally Christian eras. It was conquered by Spain's Ferdinando de León to cement the beginning of the Christian era. Recall Portugal as a country only came into being in the 12th century and was previously a "Condado" or County of León in Old Castile. King Afonso Henriques is indeed buried in one of the old monasteries in the city." (I was never quite sure where he ended up but was constantly reminded wherever we seemed to go that he got there first and captured whatever town or area from the Moslems!)

So, Coimbra is an ancient town on the Mondego River, and it looks the part. The convent and churches are on one skyline, the university on the other. The river is wide with the Santa Clara Bridge across it; the "centro" appears old and worn. It should. It took a while to warm to it after being in the several small towns the past few days. We had a fine lunch at the elegant "Dom Pedro" restaurant with a "maître" and several waiters ["senhores empregados"]. Tour crowds were just beginning to come in.

Before walking the historic center of old Coimbra and up to the university, we did a curious outing across the river to "Portugal dos Pequenos" – "Portugal for the Children." In effect it was a tiny village with miniature castles of all the architectural types of Portugal, a bit of a playground for the tots, but also a history lesson for the adults. It was built during Salazar's "Estado Novo" and finished in 1950. We found it fun and mainly clever! Adventurers all said they would have to bring the kids next time and felt like kids themselves.

After that we crossed the river, excited to move on to our main destination ...

THE UNIVERSITY OF COIMBRA

King João III, University of Coimbra

Our guide continued, "Camões in his 'Lusiads' describes its founding in the 15th century, but it was actually founded by King Dinis in Lisbon in 1290, transferred to Coimbra in 1308, back to Lisbon a bit later and made permanent in 1537 in Coimbra when King João III initiated his own palace in the university. It attracted scholars and teachers from Oxford, Paris, Salamanca and Italy and was known as a Humanist University in its earliest days.

"Originally known for the various religious faculties in the late Renaissance it became a center of science and scientific research due to the stimulus of the Marques de Pombal in the mid-18th century.

"There are currently 7,500 students; they no longer wear the long black robes associated with past times but do attach colored ribbons designating their faculties to their briefcases. They are known, among other things, for playing guitar and singing 'fados.' They live communally in 'repúblicas' of 12-13 students and hire a servant to cook for them. (I recalled the same term and custom from days in Recife, Brazil, in the 1960s.) The academic year ends in May with the 'queima das fitas' or 'the burning of the ribbons' of the graduates."

It was tough going for some of the adventurers (Amy had warned of the walk, both the grade and the cobblestones, but no one seemed to want to drop out.) One enters the University by walking through the old city with the arches in its twelfth century walls and then climbing a very steep cobblestoned street. As mentioned, it was founded in the 12th century but basic work not done on it in until the 1500s by King João III (Avis) in 1537. Luís de Camões is an alumnus as well at St. Anthony of Pádua.

THE "BIBLIOTECA GERAL"

The library constructed from 1717 to 1723 possesses the most elaborate interior architecture in all Portugal, all in the Baroque style. It was a sight to see with the gilded baroque interior by King João V; it boasts one million tomes, jade and marble floors, gilded-lacquered walls and shelves, and painted scenes on the ceiling. It is a real art gallery in itself with gorgeous rosewood and ebony tables. It seems like it would be difficult to concentrate on work with all this surrounding the reading table, but I would love to give it a try.

THE "FACULDADE DE LETRAS"

I had wanted to see the corresponding unit of the university to our "Department of Languages and Literatures" at University of Nebraska. Well, maybe not exactly since the entire system is different, following the European patterns. While most of our group headed to a quaint café in the university's main plaza for "bicas" or wine (the van back to O Porto was scheduled for 4:30 p.m.), I had an encounter with Professor João Oliveira de Lopes, Professor of Brazilian Literature, he speaking of "A Literatura Popular do Nordeste" a course just taught in 1972. When I had walked into the "Faculdade" office and introduced myself, he was called at home, rushed over and we had a pleasant but very short talk. He told of researching in Recife, knew Ariano Suassuna, Mário Souto Maior and Neuma Borges (personages of my research days in Brazil) and said all spoke well of me. He knew relatively little of Brazil's folk-popular literature, the "literatura de cordel," but I was impressed to know it was being taught at no less than Coimbra! He had used my 1973 book "A Literatura de Cordel" in the northeastern literature course. Adventurers were not present for this, oh well. It was a little like the ten minutes I and a few adventurers spent in Jorge Amado's Foundation Center in Salvador in 1973. These things happen on AT trips.

Just to close that indelible memory for me, a few hours later, at CC that night back on the ship at O Porto, one of the adventurers which some connection or other to living in Portugal spoke totally disparagingly of the "Universidade de Coimbra" as a Portuguese relic, totally out of step with modern days. Hmm. It would be interesting to see the dynamics between the Universities of Lisbon, Coimbra and O Porto. All I know is that the Universidade de Coimbra is the oldest in Portugal and dates from the times of the oldest in Europe including Oxford, Paris, Salamanca, Alcalá de Henares and perhaps Bologna. It has earned its stripes!

"IGREJA DA SÉ" – COIMBRA

After the university, on the way back down to the central plaza, on that steep cobblestone street called the "Via Latina" we and a few of the adventurer stragglers saw the old "Igreja da Sé" or Cathedral of Coimbra. A curiosity was to see a man with one leg on crutches, carrying his wooden leg in a plastic sack. You don't see that every day, pardon me, "a one – legged wonder." No criticism intended, in fact the contrary. The old "Sé" was founded in 1170. It has a Romanesque portal and on the inside rounded arches and cupola; it was built like the fortress churches of the times all over Europe and was similar to the "Sé" in Lisbon but older. The "Sé" in Lisbon is Gothic; this is Romanesque. I think it was the oldest such edifice so far in Portugal. There was a gilded Flemish "retablo" above the main altar.

THE SANTA CRUZ CHURCH – COIMBRA

We did not see this church but supposedly Affonso Henriques's sarcophagus is here, his feet resting on a lion. Someone said, "May he rest in peace. But maybe he's like Kilroy back in the U.S. Always here." There is also reference to the scene of the climax of Pedro and Ines de Castro's love story here. Two of the greatest stories of Portugal!

Final Note on Tourism in Coimbra:

Coimbra grows on you and I think I could grow to like it with the river and its traditions. We saw only one student with the formerly required black academic gown at the university, no ribbons on it at all. The guide said all the students were in exam time; there were many hundreds of graduation pictures of them in the old robes on display throughout the campus.

I confess to a nap in the coach on the two-hour drive on the expressway back to the ship. And I wasn't the only one. CC was lively (see the disparaging comment above on the University of Coimbra), but we were treated to some terrific photos and film of the naturalists' outings that day to the estuary of O Porto. Lots of libations and animated talk of the last three days, almost all positive. Surprisingly enough, many adventurers said the highlight was the wine drinking contest. All of Amy, Harry and my own hard work at culture for nothing! Chef Romano treated us to another fine dinner, and Captain Tony treated to more fine Portuguese wines, and Port after dinner. It was then an early evening for a very tired crowd, me and Amy included.

An historical note; IA, Harry decided to bypass Viana do Castelo, a small seaport in northern Portugal and also perhaps a coach ride to Guimarães, important for the birthplace of Portugal's "conquistador" and future King Affonso Henriques of Moorish conquest fame. Maybe just as well. We already had talked of his exploits and tomb, but we decided to let him rest in peace.

"Adventurer" would head due north that night and we would awake with unexpectedly rough seas rounding the northwest corner of Spain to A Coruña in Galician ["La Coruña" in Spanish], a necessary "detour" and interim in Spanish culture, but the only way we would be able to see the most important Santiago de Compostela before making the return trip two full days at sea back down to Lisbon and a surprise for all. Seasick pills were widely used; these waters were known for shipwrecks, including North Atlantic oil ships. The old Spanish Armada in 1588 a case in point.

Harry Downing took over, very much on "his turf." I knew little of the place but that "galego – português" was the language of the minority, the rest speaking Castilian or a mix of the two. Harry gave us all the details in that talk before docking in this major port.

"There was Roman occupation and development by Caesar Augustus in the 2nd century BC, little Moslem incursion this far north, but both Norman and Viking raids in the 9th century. Government was always connected to Santiago, and its Bishop reigned supreme both in politics and church affairs. There was a significant Jewish presence before 1492 with the most famous Hebrew Bible done locally.

"Atlantic trade was supreme, metals, spices and a center for textiles (there are many sheep as we would see on the road to Santiago the next day)."

Harry waxed euphoric telling of King Carlos I of Spain leaving from A Coruña to be crowned King of the Holy Roman Empire. In 1588 the Spanish Armada sailed from here in its unsuccessful attack on England. (Harry smiled.) And an old familiar figure to Spanish South America Sir Francis Drake the buccaneer (sanctioned pirate by Queen Elizabeth to "singe the beard of Hapsburg King Felipe II" attacked the port and was repelled the following year in 1589. Harry smiled again.)

Known for the Royal Dockyards, the longest maritime promenade in Europe, beaches (not for Brazilians with that icy sea), A Coruña is a tourist city in the hot peninsular summers. My studies in Spanish Literature revealed two major writers from there, Ramón Menéndez Pidal in linguistics and literature and one of Spain's best historians, Salvador de Madariaga. And Pablo Picasso lived there in the 1890s.

IA docked in rough seas and a few hardy adventurers explored the promenade and had hot chocolate or strong wine. The next day would be spectacular with travel in coaches to the most important religious site (disputed all over Spain which has many) at least for most Europeans – Santiago de Compostela and its storied history and legend of the apostle St. James.

10

SANTIAGO DE COMPOSTELA

On the road to Santiago de Compostela in Galicia they still have stone fences along wheat fields. Later the countryside became a bit bleak with rolling hills and the hand cutting of the grass or hay in the fields. There was a nice stream and they say it is trout fishing country. But the last thirty kilometers into Santiago reminded of Portugal; all was green and the vineyards were everywhere along the road. And oxen carts accompanied the cars and buses. I gave this intro on the coach:

MIKE'S HISTORY AND HIGHLIGHTS
OF SANTIAGO DE COMPOSTELA

"It is a city and region based upon legend. St. James or 'Santiago el Mayor' was believed to be the apostle of Jesus who eventually would Christianize Spain. Here's the story. Fact or legend. After the death of Jesus, he leaves Judea and arrives in the Iberian Peninsula. During a period of seven years he seems to have little success in converting the Iberians to Christianity, but then the Virgin Mary appears to him in Zaragoza, thus initiating the legend of the 'Virgin del Pilar.' He then begins to convert many people. Eventually he goes back to Judea and is killed by Herod. His disciples bring the body back to Spain to be interred. The grave is lost until the 9th century when a star leads shepherds to it. (Hmm.) In 844 A.D. King Don Ramiro I is battling the Moors at Clavijo, near Logroño. A knight on horseback with sword in hand appears, a red cross on his banner, and with his help the Spanish defeat the Moors. The knight was believed to be the apostle! As a result, St. James the Apostle becomes the patron saint of the 'Reconquista' – St. James the Moor Killer or 'Santiago Matamoros.' From the north to Granada and Sevilla!

"When the relics of St. James were discovered in the 9th century a cult arose. Its fame grew over all Europe and Santiago de Compostela in the 11th century became ranked with Rome and Jerusalem as one of three major Christian Pilgrimage sites or 'peregrinajes cristianos.' At this time the Turks controlled the eastern Mediterranean, so with that limitation in travel to Jerusalem, Santiago in what would become Spain becomes even more popular. At around this time the French united with the Spaniards and were involved with a great battle with the Moors. French, Germans, English and even Scandinavians began to make the pilgrimage to Santiago. Cities like León along the way to Santiago became famous.

"The Monastery of Compostela was originally administrated and controlled by the Benedictine and Cistercian monks and was protected by the Knights Templar – the 'Orden de la Espada Roja.' The costume or clothing of the pilgrims became a tradition: a cape, a staff, sandals and a broad brimmed hat with scallop shells on the hat, this in 1130 A.D. The 'Pilgrims' Guide' or 'Guía de Peregrinajes' at the Cathedral makes a big thing of all this.

"In medieval times there were at one time some 500,000 to two million pilgrims per year, (I myself wondered about that number) then came a gradual decline because of assault and thievery of the pilgrims along the pilgrims' route and wars between Christian countries.

"As I already mentioned, the English Corsair Sir Francis Drake armed with instructions from Queen Elizabeth to 'singe the beard of Felipe II the Spanish King' attacked nearby Coruña in 1589. The local bishop hid the relics of Santiago for fear of further attacks; they were then lost for 300 years during which the pilgrimage was abandoned.

"The relics were rediscovered in 1879 and were recognized by the Pope as legitimate, so pilgrimages started again. Plenary indulgences were given with visits during a holy year.

"There were two ways to get there — via Asturias which was dangerous and the 'Vía Francesa.'

"The Cathedral-Basilica was built on the site of the tomb. It was destroyed by the Moor Al Mansur in 997. The current Basilica dates from 11th, 12th, and 13th centuries. In 1386 John of Gaunt crowned himself King of Castile and León in the cathedral.

"So now you're ready; the guide will probably repeat all I've said. Sorry."

TOURIST HIGHLIGHTS OF SANTIAGO DE COMPOSTELA:

The "Obradeiro" Façade which is a baroque masterpiece was done in 1750. Behind the façade is the original cathedral of the Romanesque age.

The "Pórtico de la Glória," Santiago de Compostela

The "Pórtico de la Gloria" in the old cathedral is the oldest carving in the entire edifice; it is 12th century Romanesque, considered the best stone carving of medieval times in Spain. The guidebooks emphasize the personality of the figures carved and the belief and or superstition that one received good luck or a blessing by placing the imprint of the five fingers of the right hand in the proper place on the pillar before entering the church.

The "Botafumeiro" unfortunately not shown here because I do not have a photo, a huge incense boat, is used on special occasions. There is a documentary film of the mass at Santiago de Compostela with the brotherhood in action in the swinging of the huge boat. It is from two to three meters high, with an appearance like an old potbellied stove; it is attached to a very heavy rope from the ceiling above the altar and is swung back and forth at given times before, during and after mass by two or three brothers who control it with other ropes. The boat swings like a pendulum in almost the entirety of the transept of the huge church. It is finally slowed and stopped by a brother literally with a bear hug. The saying is that the incense was needed to fill the church thus hiding the stench of all those dirty, sweaty pilgrims in attendance.

The high altar in the center of the nave with its 13th century statue of Santiago the Apostle is sumptuous and some say "gaudy" in appearance. It was completed in true Baroque style and splendor in the 16th century. Some say it all is a "baroque monstrosity." One can go through a small corridor behind the main altar and touch (or kiss) the mantle of the image of the saint. Under the altar is a tomb constructed with the remains of the 9th century church; it is believed to contain the bones of the saint himself. Whew!

SOCIALIZING IN SANTIAGO DE COMPOSTELA

On the first night in Santiago de Compostela most of us went to the Plaza de España with the huge cathedral, the "ayuntamiento," and the Hotel - Parador. There were drinks of "Ribeiro Claro," like the "Vinho Verde of Portugal," and "caldo galego" at "Fornas" Restaurant.

The next a.m. was the official tour. Afterwards Amy and I investigated the great national "Parador," the "Rey Fernando" just off the huge plaza on one side. There was a chance encounter with the familiar "tunas" or student musical groups throughout much of Spain. The long black academic robes and accompanied ribbons were impressive. They offered cassete tapes of their recordings for sale. That night was a time of a big party or "noche de parranda" with a big crowd. There was "Vino Ribeiro, caldo gallego, y pimiento," singing with the "tunas," the students from Navarra, and the party continued with adventurers in a local hotel. The next day all felt a bit for the worse.

There had been mass in the Cathedral in the earlier p.m. That was when we saw the aforementioned huge incense boat or "bota fumeiro."

A note on language from our guide Marcela Alarcón, a native of Santiago de Compostela: "Galego – Português" is spoken now by only one third of the population; most speak Castilian. When she gave us an example (requested by yours truly), I understood only a few words and even the Portuguese crowd said they got only about one half (figures, huh? galego – português). She did her guiding in English and I only got half of that too.

After those two full days in this wonderful small city it was back to the coaches and the ride to La Coruña, on board IA and most adventurers glad to be "at home" out of the cold and rain. CC that night was a hoot! Harry's commentary was entertaining; he said we should all be happy that the Virgen María does not have to carry the entire load for getting rid of those nasty Moors and, as per the case, Spanish or Portuguese crusaders for that matter – St. James on the white horse helped a bit. The same adventurer who said earlier in the trip he was tired of all the "Catholic nonsense" spoke up again, saying, "Thank God back in Cleveland we don't have to hear this horse shit." That caused some "Yankee go home" remarks, but Harry diffused the situation with a pithy remark, "You may have knock – knock jokes in Cleveland, but our neighbors in Ireland have Our Lady of Knock, so I guess we are even. And sorry to say, you are immensely outnumbered; the pilgrims from all over Christian Europe, from Scandinavia to Andalusia, have been making the trek to Compostela for at least ten centuries. And I understand hundreds of thousands of your people do the "Way of Santiago" just for the hike of it (I meant "heck of it"), that plus the wine stations in the hostels along the way where they are known for easing their pain. We in Europe call it 'trekking,' and, besides, you get a free ticket to heaven if you complete the entire Way of Santiago – one of those 'Plenary Indulgences' still granted by our Friend in Rome! (Peals of laughter from the crowd.) It makes up for the blisters on one's feet." The Cleveland joker would not let up, "If you go twice is it two trips to heaven or can you bring a friend along?" Harry said, "If your jokes have two knocks, not much sense is there to one? The matter will be up to that bureaucratic secretary in that dingy office or orifice in the wall in Santiago who stamps your 'Way of Santiago Passport.' She will make the decision; I assume there is a direct line to Rome in case of contingencies. Most Catholics I know tend to commit the same sins over and over, ergo, a new confession and perhaps a new Indulgence. By the way we in the Church of England did not discard that custom; *we* even sold them for a while!" Such back and forth spiced up many a CC and more to come I surmise. Oh, by the way, I would have a conversation with Mr. Owens of Cleveland and ask him some questions. But that would be later.

I don't know if adventurers were tired of it but Chef Reynaldo served "caldo Gallego" that night – delicious! And hot! Plus copious amounts of Vino Ribeiro. It seemed to ease the pain of the pilgrimage. Then for most it was reminiscing and to bed early for the big day tomorrow.

Amy and I that night replayed the tit for tat – and we both agreed with, who is it, Pascal? To hedge our bets. What do they call it? Pascal's Wager about the existence of God. You do or you don't, so why not hedge, if … or … if not. It would be immensely nice if Santiago's remains *are* buried beneath that monstrosity of a gold altar. I did pat the back side of the statue of St. James in that passageway behind the main altar. How can I say this without being vulgar (oh go ahead Gaherty), I did not kiss the statue as did many. So did Amy and for that matter everyone else. But … no indulgence!

I would be giving details of tomorrow evening's festivities, along with AAL Amy tomorrow morning at 10:00 a.m.

11

AT SEA, OVERNIGHT TO LISBON

It was around 390 nautical miles, at top speed, 17 hours, so IA would travel during the night and dock around 1 p.m., do bureaucracy and then Chico and Maricta on board for CC, dinner and small concert; off ship that night. I was up early making notes for the short intro to Chico Buarque along with Amy. We did it in her room for privacy for her from normal ship interruptions.

Many adventurers knew all about Chico Buarque and his musical (and political) fame in Brazil. The handful who were on the "Around Brazil" trip in 1973 had also heard him perform. I did the background notes (like for an LP) and Amy the logistics.

"Chico Buarque is Brazil's most popular and most sophisticated composer and singer. His seven-year career has been spectacular, winning the national song competition on the old "Música Popular Brasileira" back in 1966 and 1967 with "A Banda" ["The Band"] a song still epitomizing carnival in Rio. His early sambas have evolved to sophisticated tunes with double entendre lyrics adapting to the atmosphere of "pre – censorship" by the military regime. Yours truly has known him since 1971 when I did research on two or three of his songs related to famous Northeastern music and the folk – popular poetry of Brazil, a long story. I had the good fortune to play and sing along with him in 1971 in a concert called 'Memories of Our Youth' when he did a reprise of his teenage favorite Rock n' Roll songs from the U.S. and his early samba. We then did no less than three big concerts, two in Rio, one at Itaipu Dam with the theme of encouraging Brazilian job development at the time. An unfortunate political event, the imprisonment and torture of one of Brazil's biggest voices for political reform, brought the concerts to a halt. Chico since has been largely curtailed from composing and performing in Brazil.

"But the Brazilian military recalled his wonderful and successful performance on IA in Rio in 1973 and granted him permission for a one — time concert in Lisbon where most love him. We get a 'side' performance on ship tomorrow night. I'll join him in the lounge where we'll sing old U.S. Rock n' Roll and his early sambas. His beautiful wife Marieta will be along; their second time on IA. I can only say we are highly privileged for this to happen. Come ready to tap your toes to the music. Amy's got the nuts and bolts for the evening for us."

"Hi adventurers. I am so excited for this to happen I'm about to bust my buttons (Willie said later, "That would have been a treat!"). Like Mike said, I was aboard IA in 1973 and helped set up the whole thing, a major entertainment 'scoop' for us at the time. This is no less. Chico and Marieta speak English, their native language of course is Brazilian Portuguese, but both know Spanish and a significant amount of Italian. They will join us in the lounge at 5:30 for cocktails, be Captain Tony's guests at dinner and the 'show' will be back in the lounge at 8:00 p.m. We can help Chico out by buying some of his LPs and cassetes. He will have just concluded two shows for the general public in Lisbon and will fly out tomorrow for Rio. Dress up a bit and put on your dancing shoes."

I added, "The say gringos can't dance samba, I know I can't. But Amy can and our barman Dimitri will have plenty of Brazilian 'caipirinhas' to loosen us up. After maybe three we'll all be dancing to Chico's cassetes on the music system. See you there."

Maurício Salazar stood up, and in a very loud voice said, "We old timers from the old days in Portugal, I mean before 1974, have a bone to pick with Chico for one of his songs. But that's water under the bridge; in this case we will let bygones be bygones because everything else will be great."

Later that morning, seas had calmed, weather was beautiful and we chugged into the Tejo Estuary, then past Cascais and Belém into the docks at Lisbon; most adventurers out on deck to see that marvelous sight and traveling past the old fort, the monastery, and the huge July 25th Bridge and back to the familiar dock near the Praça do Paço. There was time for a short excursion on shore for shopping, seeing any "old favorites" and back to the ship by 4:00 and preparation for Chico and Marieta.

Chico, Marieta and three of his band came on board at 4:30; we all were there to greet them, me, Amy, Captain Tony. Lots of "abraços, beijos" and such. Chico embraced me saying, "O' Arretado, we meet again. This is special; we have only good memories. You seem to be doing well since Brazil, a lot to catch up on." Marieta hugged Amy, then me, and we greeted the musicians and backup singer Gini. Crew helped them to their "staging room," then to the lounge for set up and drinks. I had not forgotten that Chico liked his "cachaça and caipirinhas," so that was what we started with, barman Dimitri doing his best in a Brazilian imitation.

Chico and I had a lot to catch up on; he wanted to know what all I was up to since 1973, so he got the whole story of the Mexico escapades with Amy in 1974, the IA trip to Mexico in 1975, "Around Brazil" again in 1976, and now here in Portugal and Spain. Talking in Portuguese, he wanted to know, ahem, whether I was still in contact with "old friends" in Brazil, meaning Cristina Maria. And he knew about Molly, but Amy was right next to me on the divan so what could I say? "Não Chico, Amy me ocupa totalmente agora!" We all laughed, and then my turn for questions: "novidades" in Brazil, and how was the concert in Lisbon?

"O mesmo, o mesmo no Brasil. Depois de 'Cálice,' e você sabe aquela história (Li 'Letters from Brasil III' e você acertou!) a vida profissional muito reduzida. A vida agora é muito como "Deus lhe Pague." Ha. Ha. E devemos muito a você, Amy e Capitão Antônio pela 'santa intercessão' pelo evento em Portugal." [The same, the same ole' thing. After "Cálice," ["Chalice, or Be Silent"] and you know that story (I read "Letters from Brazil III" and you got it right!) professional life is very reduced. Life now is like I described in 'Deus lhe Pague.' Ha ha. And we owe a lot to you, Amy and Captain Antônio for the 'holy intercession' to get the event in Portugal."] The two concerts in Lisbon have helped the pocketbook, and you could tell the crowd, almost all young Lisboetas favoring the 1974 Revolution, still liked us. I led off each night with "Tanto Mar" ["So Much Sea"] and a wonderful reception, then we did a pot pourri of the old stuff. There were protestors from the "old guard" outside the venue, but aside from some boos and posters, no problem. Let's drink up, 'Tim tim' to the present."

Marieta caught us up with the kids, now finishing "colégio" and prepping for the "vestibular" or college entrance exam. "DOPS agents in front of the house and up on Chico's walking trail up to the forest in Tijuca, and frankly, Chico in a bit of a funk (which he sadly nodded his head, agreeing). But old friends stick by us, Jobim, Vinicius de Morais, Nara Leão and Milton Nascimento."

Chico added, "I've been composing but not recording and have a whole drawer full of lyrics and melodies. Things are loosening up a bit – municipal and state elections allowed by the military and some signs of good things to come. So keep going to mass and praying for a political opening; the Church and Cardinal Arns in São Paulo have been the only voices really allowed for freedom. Oh, and for your memories, Itaipu Dam is full steam ahead, and the Transamazonic Highway rolls on through that muck and mud up north. But Carnival is still wonderful, 'futbol' is great, and they can't close the beaches."

Some adventurers, timid at first, crowded in, took pictures and were busy buying LPs and cassetes which one of the band members was selling at the side. We then filed in to a scrumptious dinner, Brazilian favorites with an Italian flourish, and good Portuguese (sorry, no Brazilian) wines. It was hard to have complete privacy; Leonel came by, gave a warm hello, and reminded Chico he knew his father the Historian and his uncle, the Linguist (author of Brazil's best-known Portuguese dictionary) quite well, and wished us all well. Even Maurício Salazar stopped by, saying in

Portuguese of course that he has all the albums but detests that one song; "You know which one." When Chico was introduced and knowing now of the Salazar connection, he just said, "Sinto muito Maurício, os tempos passam, as águas rolam. [I'm sorry Maurício, times change, the rivers roll on.] But that song is more about how I felt in Brazil at the time, and by the way, didn't you like the musical accompaniment? I think anyone from Portugal would want to dance!" Maurício retorted, "Let's cut the lyrics and leave the rest! Ha ha." It was all amicable.

So, now for the festivities. For my old readers it's a bit of a reprise from on board from 1973. For the new folks, I'll repeat a bit so all can understand what we were up to. The "cordel" has a whole series of story – poems which treat the migration of poor northeasterners to Brazil's south, and Chico had a great song "Pedro Pedreiro" ["Pete the Laborer"] coincidentally telling of the migrant's life in São Paulo and his hopes of returning home in the Northeast. I interviewed Chico back in 1970 on it; we clicked, and after drinking a lot of beer and cachaça, accidentally talked of his old love for U.S. Rock n' Roll. That evolved to a fun time of both of us playing and singing the songs, Chico's impulsive idea to do a recording of the same, done deal, and concerts with that stuff and Chico's early days. The rest is history. The concerts, then a political explosion, all abruptly halted by the military and their 'request' for me to leave Brazil. Our reunion on IA in 1973 and now again in Lisbon.

So I joined Chico and the band, we sang the old Rock n' Roll, then Chico reprised his old melodic sambas including "A Banda." All to applause and some dancing. Chico looked at me, "Tanto Mar?'" I nodded yes and the band played it, the adventurers not getting the lyrics, but loving the melody. Here's part of it:

> … Eu queria estar na festa, Pá; Com tua gente
> I wanted to be at the party, Pá; With all your people
> E colher pessoalmente, uma flor de teu jardim
> And to personally pick, a flower from your garden

> Sei que há léguas de nos separar, Tanto Mar Tanto Mar
> I know there are leagues separating us, So much sea, so much sea
> Sei também que é preciso Pá, Navegar, Navegar. …
> I also know that it's necessary, Pá, Navigate, Navigate.

All the adventurers were on their feet, dancing to that wonderful Portuguese melody and rhythm. And standing applause. Chico smiled; I smiled. Maurício stood with his hands up, thumbs down, but then joining the applause. "Sucesso!" I can only add for you adventurers that the song expressed in the first verse Chico's congratulations for the Revolution of the Flowers in 1974, his sadness not to be able to join them in the euphoric moment, but at least to receive a carnation as a remembrance. And the last verse, Chico being "sick" in Brazil but at least wanting to smell the flowers. All this is controversial, in opposition to the old Salazar regime, suggesting the happiness at its demise, but most of all, sadness that Brazil could not have the same!

Chico then quickly closed repeating "A Banda," all danced, and then the bar opened, drinks on the house, autographs and happiness. Amy and my fears of any further negative response happily did not come to pass. An hour later, the party over, we said our goodbyes, embraces and a few tears, Chico and Marieta and the band thanking us profusely (Amy slipping a performance check into his hands) and we said our goodbyes, both of us wishing for coming good days for Brazil. Wow! A moment to be remembered by all. And a footnote: almost unanimous thanks for the moment and even the pro – Salazar contingent admitting that some good things do come from Brazil.

Amy and I had a late meeting in her room, still wired from it all, but happy. She said, "It's like old times. We should have the same. And we did."

12

SOUTH TO THE ALGARVE AND GOODBYE TO PORTUGAL

As we awoke the next morning, Captain Tony was keeping IA fairly close to shore running past the scary cape of São Vicente and Sagres, and then the gorgeous beaches at the "cape" of Portugal in the Algarve. The fact is that the beaches would run along the entire south coast and the best place to dock would be Lagos. In an unusual moment, both Captain Tony and Exec Martim would accompany vans from Lagos to the windswept point of Sagres, the most important place in Portugal for seafarers in the 15th century. At least in legend. Why? The maritime school and the main place of unsung heroes – the mapmakers of Portugal. And the school of navigation. Both Tony and Martim were graduates of the modern Naval School of Alfeite, on the south bank of the Tague at Lisbon, but all Portuguese sailors, naval officers and seafarers remembered their history! An option for that morning and all joining in the p.m. were the wonderful beaches of the Algarve. The true historic port however was Lagos where Henrique the Navigator spent most of his time, and from this port the caravels moved on to explore and to enrich Portugal with the gold of Africa and then the Far East (but the later expeditions left from Lisbon).

Captain Tony became the guide as the coach came into the windswept remains of Sagres with the dangerous high cliffs of the coast to the west.

We saw the point, the remains of the historic fort built by Henry, ruined by the earthquake of 1755, the huge pebble compass and the small local church. Captain Tony gave the spiel:

"Sagres is bathed in legend but perhaps not mixed with reality. The legend first: Henry the Navigator established a school of navigation and an observatory on the point where seafarers were trained in the same, and maps were drawn for Portugal's imminent conquest of the seas. The belief that Portugal's greatest riches were at first *not* the gold to come from Africa nor the spices of the Far East, but the *maps* drawn in Sagres guarded more closely than the King's treasure house. He did construct an important fort that guarded the promontory and Cape São Vicente for centuries. The facts: the real center of navigation and sailing was the port of Lagos where we docked.

"King João I assembled his fleet to attack (and conquer) Ceuta in Morocco from Lagos in 1471, the first huge step in the circumnavigation of Africa years later by Bartolomeu Dias. Then came the discoveries of gold in Africa with Lagos the main port receiving them. And, unhappily, the huge slave trade that Portugal would exploit for centuries, most famously later in Brazil. But Lagos dimmed as the 15th century wore on and Lisbon took its place, what we have all seen."

Adventurers dragged in that p.m., most from a mid – June day at the wonderful beaches, a few sunburned, and all ready for our final CC in Portugal. It's on to Spain tomorrow and another reality. It was tying up loose ends with Harry in charge, and he did not disappoint. (He also planned for his own introduction to Spain tomorrow morning and with me a short introduction to our first stop – Málaga and Then three days in Andalucía.)

"Well, ladies and gentlemen. Part I of our expedition draws to a close. I hope you all have enjoyed it. It *has* been a lively group I must say. A bit of, how do you Americans say, "The Hatfields and the McCoys," but Portuguese style, and we staff I think performed our role as referees, perhaps not so much as in a football match, certainly not Rugby, although I feared a scrum here in the lounge (laughter), but rather a small disagreement like in cricket I think. Our friends from India would probably agree. (Applause and laughter.) We were all gentlemanly about it most of the time. (More laughter.) I don't think anyone can deny the marvelous places we saw, the good food we enjoyed, and the wine imbibed as well. Being a Brit, I'll still take Port, but I realize that is a bit strong for those of you across the pond.

"A special round of applause for Eli for providing so much wonderful music, and to Amy and Mike for that Brazilian touch the last night in Lisbon (he did not go on about Chico Buarque, exercising a clever managerial decision I thought). But even more to our Captain Antônio and crew for wheeling us up and down, hither and yon, seeing the highlights of Portugal. We can all reminisce a bit for another hour, and then one more, can you imagine it, repast from Chef Reynaldo, and then you are on your own for the evening. Tomorrow morning at 9:00 I shall introduce you to a rather abbreviated plan for what is to come. España! From my experience it will indeed be quite different from Portugal; there is no ancient Anglo – Portuguese diplomatic treaty to discuss, but a totally, in my view, new outlook and flavor of life. Thank you. See you tomorrow a.m."

It was a lively rest of CC, lots of reminiscing, some questions (in private conversation of course) about me and Amy, talk of past trips on IA, that sort of thing. I have not said much about the Spain "aficionados" aboard but there are many, mostly adventurers just wanting to see more of that fabled country. There will be, like Portugal, some with family ties to Spain (Rachel among them), and some with strong opinions of the old Franco days and now the "new dawn" with King Juan Carlos and Queen Sophia. More on that to come.

PART II - SPAIN

13

PASSING GIBRALTAR TO MÁLAGA

Early that morning IA passed Gibraltar and Harry got on the speaker phone which caught our attention. "Adventurers, through the haze and fog you see a large rock; that's the closest we shall get to anything Britannic the rest of this trip. It used to be called 'the Pillars of Hercules' and is a strategic spot for both commercial and military reasons, taking into account Africa is through the haze far to the south. The 'Pillars' legend is just that, going back to the ancient Greeks and then the Romans, something about Hercules hunting for lost cattle (that's a joke for those in the know). Way back when, at the beginning of the 1700s there was something called 'The War for Spanish Succession' with three different figures vying for the kingship of Spain (vacant due to a lack of inheritors of the crown) with different countries of Europe siding with each one. It was a bit like a big prize fight, but with three pugilists. England came out okay with possession of the Rock and the tiny town of Gibraltar which remains under English sovereignty today with referendums as common as afternoon tea, or so it seems, and always massively favoring staying with Britain. Just thought you would like to know."

IA was moving along slowly early in the day to give us time for preliminaries. That first a.m. was dedicated to Harry's introduction to Spain and my introduction to Málaga. Harry first.

"This will be short just to get the ball rolling. Spain was originally occupied by the "Íberos" or Iberian peoples. But there were many original visitors, commercial at first on the south coast, then conquerors. We had the Phoenicians, those sea faring commercial endeavors, Hannibal and Carthage and his battle against Rome, but it was the Romans who came and conquered. It's a long story, and our friend Caesar Augustus eventually made it all the way to Gaul and Britain, but Rome's presence was omniscient through most of Spain. They established outposts, then forts and colonies all through what we shall see the next few days – Andalusia, the Roman capital at Córdoba, but also Seville and Málaga. They would reach up to central Spain in Salamanca, Cáceres, and Segovia, and had an important presence in Zaragoza ("César Augusto"). You may recall the apostle St. James's important moments, at least according to legend, in the latter place. And it was they who would bring law and most importantly their language, Latin, perhaps Vulgar Latin at that, to Spain. The Romance Languages are derived from that, in this case and in many evolved forms, Spanish or as they say here, "Castellano.""

"The Moors would come from 711 to 1492, almost 800 years of domination, early peace and progress, then continued battles with the Spanish knights such as El Cid (you recall the shmaltzy movie with Charlton Heston and Sophia Loren, what unlikely Spaniards they were! But hooray for Hollywood!). The Moors were finally conquered near here in Granada in 1492, Columbus discovered America, and the Edict of Granada changed Spain forever with the expulsion or forced conversions of the defeated Moslems and, incidentally, the Jews. That was when modern Spain really began, the unification of the independent areas under the Catholic Kings Fernando and Isabella (Aragón and Castille). The rest is modern history. And we shall see a good bit of it. Now Michael will get us off to a rollicking start with Málaga."

"AT will give IA a rest, a refitting in the yards at Málaga while we do what is called a "gira" or tour of Andalusia. Vans, hotels and guides will take us for four days, after Málaga, to Córdoba, Granada and Sevilla. AT mainly Amy has set up great guides, coaches and top flight accommodations. The Paradores! So enjoy our hospitality these two full days in Málaga and ship board amenities before our 'Gira.' "Gracias.'"

Then it was my turn to prep all for the two more full days in this delightful, a bit touristy, but important Andalusian city.

MIKE'S INTRODUCTION TO MÁLAGA

The Port, City of Málaga

"Málaga is a city and a municipality, capital of the Province of Málaga in the modern parlance 'Autonomous Community of Andalusia.' One of the oldest cities in the western world, it was founded by the Phoenicians and was under the power of ancient Carthage! It then came under Roman rule and after them Islamic domination for eight hundred years. In 1487 it came under Christian rule again. It is perhaps best known in modern times as the birthplace of Pablo Picasso. Yours truly can attest to its amazing

Spanish Classic Guitar heritage with the entire Romero family which was forced to migrate from Málaga during Franco days to the United States. We have the Generalísimo to thank for this! We will have vans and the local guides to help us; AL Harry and I will be along. 'Buen viaje'

FIRST DAY IN SPAIN AT MÁLAGA

The Virgin and the Black Christ, Málaga

Okay, we are in Spain and Málaga first, so it's main "centro" and a church. Our first among many, one of the options was the noon mass at the Cathedral of Málaga. For those of you of a more secular bent there was the famous "Paseo Público," a bit like "Las Ramblas" in Barcelona to come. The cathedral was huge, a combination of Romanesque, Gothic and Baroque. We also noticed its statues of the Black Christ and the elegant Virgin Mary, organ music, singing and afterwards the huge Corpus Christi procession. The Cathedral dates from the 16th century and the choir and choir stalls in beautifully carved wood come from the 17th. That morning for the mass the Cathedral was jammed. The priest droned on for about fifty minutes about Corpus Christi and Caritas! Good thing the "secular" adventurers were not there. The P.A. system was good, and his Spanish was slow and beautiful, the clearest I have heard here –that of an "Obispo." The organ in the Málaga Cathedral was nice and there was some singing as well.

Silver Monstrance, Corpus Christi, Málaga

Okay, the truth. We left mass early not because of the clarity of the priest's diction but due to the previously alluded to fifty-minute sermon. Outside the church doors we were facing the Bishop's palace in front of the cathedral and saw the huge silver and gold monstrance carried in the Corpus Christi procession. Thousands of people were milling about, winding through the downtown area in the procession. There was a military band, banners, priests and mainly the monstrance. I surmise this is a bit like Holy Week or "Semana Santa." Another moment of good fortune on the calendar, but Amy admitted this one she had not surmised ahead of time.

Later that first afternoon we leisurely walked through "Paseo Público" park in Málaga and saw our 'unofficial greeter,' a 'burrico' made of metal and its ears all shiny from all that rubbing the brass for good luck. We walked with adventurers along the quay to the Parola and Malagueta area of beach and the ocean. We noted the big billboards with advertisements for the upcoming "Feria" or Festival. AT and Amy had planned this time for such things. It wasn't far to the historic "alcazaba" or Moorish palace, but at least so far, not matching Portugal!

I neglected to mention one important item on that "paseo" – some of us left the others in the cafés along the "Paseo," but a handful including yours truly made one quick stop a few blocks away. There was the house of Pablo Picasso who was born in 1881 and lived in Málaga ten years before the family moved to Galicia and later Barcelona. More important, can that be, for music lovers – nearby, the house, birthplace and residence of the famous Romero family, "The Royal Family of the Spanish Guitar." Celedonio the 'Pater Familias" with Ángel, Celín and Pepe were all born in Spain and moved with the family to the U.S. in 1957, the father citing concern over Francisco Franco's suspicion of artists. I saw them twice at the auditorium on the U. of N. campus and was awed by both the flamenco and the classical music. They in fact became models for my amateur playing of the Renaissance Lute Suite.

It was here I reencountered an adventurer from way back in 1973, the lady conductor of symphonic orchestras throughout the world. She reminisced over conducting the "Concierto de Aranjuez," really the most important for guitar, but that it created all kinds of technical difficulties. Guitars simply do not have the volume to compete with an orchestra and amplification is necessary. "Either that or sometimes I had to tone down the orchestra so much it really spoiled the piece." But her favorite guitarist was Narciso Yepes; we talked of course of Andrés Segovia the old master and innovator from Spain and I got to tell of hearing him just once in concert in Lincoln, he now more than 80 years old. I recall him seating himself on the straight back chair and rocking back and forth to get his foot stool where he wanted it! Once he settled down the eighty years did not matter, and J. S. Bach was his favorite that night.

So that first night we all went to the "Malagueta" festival with the ladies in flamenco-style dresses, a street dance atmosphere, but now with the true "ambiente" of Spain! This now seemed to be what we expected to see - the "real" Spain! It was impressive! Part of the "feria" or "fiesta" would be the series of major bullfights held in Spain at the Malagueta arena. A long, long day but thrilling.

DAY TWO IN THE A.M. BEACH
SCENE AT TORREMOLINOS

This morning Amy and I piled into AT vans with the adventurers to Torremolinos – the town and the beach. The van ride was totally unimpressive; the countryside was dry, brown, bleak and with lots of trash along the highway until we entered the town. Once we arrived at the ocean then there was a resort atmosphere all the way. I cannot compare the scene and experience to the French or Italian Rivieras because I've never been there, but suspect they are quite similar. Most of the adventurers indeed could compare and were a bit reticent saying yes, the French and Italian beach towns were better. In Torremolinos the atmosphere exudes sun, sex and pleasure! What else? The beach was brown sand and with rock pebbles, not quite what I was used to in Acapulco or the shores of Brazil, or for that matter, Nazaré and the Algarve in Portugal, but the water was a beautiful turquoise, calm with nary a wave, incredibly so for a "sea."

There were paddle boats like on the Russian Postcards of the Black Sea Resorts. The water was icy cold! I did get in all the way but could not bear it for long, so it was no fun to swim. The big story for us was that the beach was topless! Indeed, we saw some nice boobs, mainly English and Scandinavian I think, judging from the top of the head and down! Lady adventurers were a bit reluctant to join in! Maurício Salazar was scandalized, "We don't allow this in Portugal!" Amy in her green bikini just laughed but agreed such sights should be more private.

My stomach was upset (not for the first time) so at lunch I had Spanish "tortilla" or potato, good for the stomach they say. Adventurers had paella and were happy with it. Later we all had huge "sangria" drinks and watched bits of a bullfight on television. It was a good TV introduction to Spain! Later in the p.m. many of us would see the real thing in the beautiful, classic "plaza de toros" near the anchorage of the IA.

This bullfight was held in conjunction with the "Feria Malagueta" in those somewhat hectic days. Walking to the entrance and buying our tickets, another aspect of the "Malagueta" Festival which we were indeed fortunate to see was in the streets where there were beautiful Andalusian horses with the "caballeros" in their flat brimmed hats and the ladies riding side saddle in their flamenco dresses. This of course is the area of Spain famous for blue blooded horses and people who know how to train and ride them. The famous Arabians!

How can I say it, the bull fight had its pros and cons. This was not yet in major bull fight season albeit the "Feria" celebration. We saw the "toreros" for the bull fight in their "traje de luces" arriving in carriages on the way to the Plaza. This turned out not to be a major event; it was a small-time amateur bullfight featuring the "escuela taurina" or bullfighting academy. It was a school for both the students and very young bulls – these were the real stock but were not full grown and heavy, and their horns were filed down. The music was the accustomed of the bull fight and was moving in that sense.

The "Malagueta" arena is "classic" in shape with "small" boxes on the upper decks and the "sol y sombra" section on concrete steps below. The crowd was tiny, the "picador" was used only slightly; no one could get the "banderillas" placed. A young girl or "toreadora" came in and was tossed by the bull on the first "paso." This amateur experience perhaps gives perspective to one of the serious ones I had the good fortune to see in of all places along the Mexico-U.S. border in Arizona, i.e. el Cordobés en Nogales, México.

An aside is permitted on bull fighting with the premise that this author is by no means an expert, but I am a fan. I've seen the old classic black and white film on "El Gran Manolete" and others, but for my generation the most famous "torero" in all Spain was "El Cordobés." One of the best books I have seen on the art of bull fighting is "Or I'll Dress You in Mourning" and is the biography of El Cordobés. Notwithstanding accounts by Ernest Hemingway, Gerald Brenan or James Michener, it is like nothing else I have ever read, and I recommended it in every Spanish culture class I taught so far at the university. To make a long story short, at the height of his success El Cordobés was enticed by some wealthy entrepreneurs to bring his talents to Mexico, but to an unusual venue – he was hired to do a series of bullfights in various border town arenas in the late 1960s - Ciudad Juárez, Nogales, Arizona, and Tijuana in California among them. I and friends did a long drive to Nogales and witnessed a true spectacle. Not only did he shine that afternoon, receiving six ears if I am not mistaken, but did something that forever is in my mind: he did a series, many "pasos" or passes on his knees with his back to the bull, an unimaginably daring feat.

That night in Málaga we were exhausted, but showered and dressed and went down to the "Malagueta" Festival again. This time there was blaring, unbearable disco music on the main street and blaring "sevillana" and "flamenco" music elsewhere – it was a true street dance in southern Spain. There were dozens of girls in flamenco dresses dancing with the men, all doing graceful "sevillanas," a dance it was a real pleasure to watch.

We were all weary to bed on our last night aboard IA; tomorrow the "gira" would begin, four intensive days seeing the best of Andalusia. Harry commented that this trip, especially from now on, would be a slight departure from AT's normal, mainly seafaring and expeditions on shore, but in his opinion perhaps more intellectually "fulfilling." Amy had done hours of preparation and was exhausted; she said this now would be her "vacation."

14

ADVENTURERS' "GIRA" BEGINS

To make sense of it all, historically that is, we have to do it chronologically, thus Córdoba, then Granada, and finally Sevilla "to seal the deal." Our reunion with IA will be in four or five days. Because all adventurers are on the "gira," it's three coaches to Córdoba. Here's what happened. Harry and I are along with the guides. I'll report what I saw and some interesting sidelines.

CÓRDOBA

Day Trip to Córdoba

Córdoba rests on the west bank of the Guadalquivir River. Its history goes way back, all the way to Roman Baética in 152 B.C when it shortly thereafter became the Roman capital of Hispania; we noted the Roman Bridge over the river. All was compressed into a day trip, intensive but great! The town is inseparable from its literary figures: this was the birthplace of both Sénecas from the first century A.D.: Séneca the Rhetorician of 55 B.C. and his son Lucas Séneca the philosopher and Preceptor of Nero from 4 B.C. to 65 A.D. According to one source Nero named him a Consul and also commanded him to commit suicide! Lucanus of Córdoba was a companion to Nero. Centuries later in safer times, relatively speaking, the Spanish Baroque poet and "prince of darkness" Luis de Góngora was from here as well."

As we were all stopped at the entrance to the bridge and listening to the guide's explanation, a very striking woman came up to me, although with a sad demeanor. She said, "Pardon me Professore Miguel, there has been no opportunity to introduce myself before, I'm not really sure why that did not happen. I am Sophia Pagello and I'd love to talk to you at dinner soon and we can get acquainted. Suffice to say right now that I'm from Florence and very happy now to see that your expedition is showing something that my countrymen, albeit, Classical Roman, contributed to the Peninsula. I know you talked of Romans in Portugal, but this is truly a spectacular work in evidence. This is just one of the reasons I'm on the trip, but more on that later."

"Sophia, molto piacere e grazie (my Italian is non − existent, almost). I'm happy to have your acquaintance and there's much more to come for you, really all over Spain, but especially in places like Cáceres with the amphitheater and Segovia with the aqueduct and another bridge in Salamanca. Let's talk more soon. Oh, are you traveling with others from Florence?"

"Unhappily no, but many of your adventurers have made me feel welcome."

"I'll try to do the same. We'll talk soon."

The guide talked non − stop on the bridge and later in the parking lot crammed with coaches, this before we actually visited the Mosque.

"In 719 A.D. the Emirs from the Damascus Caliphate migrated here and set up a new caliphate. The Umayyad dynasty would rule for 300 years with great prosperity and high culture. In 929 A.D. the caliphate in Spain is declared independent from Damascus. In 1000 the caliphate crumbles into what became separate Moorish Kingdoms − the 'Taifas.' The area was called 'Al Andalus.' Córdoba then fell under the rule of Sevilla until the 12th century when the Christians conquered.

"In 1126 to 1198 it is the time of the Moorish scholar Averroes, famous for his learning and for the teachings and writings of Aristotle he brought to the West. Then it is the time of Maimónides 1135-1204: a Jewish scholar of medicine and philosophy. (An aside: the guidebook said there are only 15,000 Jews in modern Spain.)

"Cristóbal Colón received permission here in Córdoba from the 'Reyes Católicos' to do the voyage to the West. 'El Gran Capitán,' Gonzalo Fernández de Córdoba (1453-1515) was the general of the Catholic Kings who carried out the conquest of Córdoba and later captured Naples as well in 1504. The 'Mesquita de Córdoba' was the high point of Caliphate art begun in the middle of the 8th century, augmented by later kings and finished in the 10th century."

"Here we go."

Entrance to the Mosque of Córdoba

One enters through the Mesquita through "La Puerta del Perdón" and enters the Court of the Orange Trees ["Naranjos"]. The outside of the mosque is plain with a brick wall. There were fountains and baths to wash in, thus purifying oneself before entering the temple – the best known called the Al Mansur Basin.

The mosque is overlooked by the Minaret; some of us later would climb its stairway to see a great view of the river and the city from there. The Arabs bought the location, razed the old Visigothic Christian church and began building in many phases: 785, 848, 961 and 987.

Interior of the Mosque of Córdoba

They used the old marble columns from previous churches and raised in the Mesquita a massive number of columns. These are double arched (one arch on top of the other; the red and white color is from the stone alternated with red brick). The original aisles were open to the court. The Christians closed in the arches later. The Mihrab is the highly ornamented chapel of the Caliphs, similar in style to that coming up in the Alhambra but done years earlier.

In the 16th century during the reign of Carlos V in 1523 the Spaniards cut away the center of the Mosque to build a church vault and cupola. When Carlos V saw this in the 1520s, he was shocked and dismayed and stopped further construction. It was completed later. The Church is Gothic (1520-1547), Renaissance (the 1560s) and Italian (1598). The dome and the Baroque choirs with pulpits which date from 1760 are all done in dark mahogany. This was the same wood as used in the pulpit.

The great irony: the Christian practice during the "Reconquista" was to destroy all mosques and build Catholic cathedrals in their place. This great mosque was saved only because the Catholic Cathedral was built inside. History is a witness to its uniqueness: two faiths under one roof. It was impressive for its size, the beauty of Moslem design and also the combination of Christian designs in the cathedral. For me (after seeing the Alhambra) it was the contrast that made it most interesting.

As we were walking from the Mesquita an adventurer I had seen but never had a chance to meet or talk to came up and said, "Mike, can we take a break and have a small conversation?" Fine. There was a coffee shop nearby so I invited him and we had a very interesting talk. He introduced himself as Faisal Rahman, his taken Muslim name, his former, Joseph Randall, of Philadelphia.

"Professor Miguel, first of all, I have thoroughly enjoyed the trip, all those historic and beautiful places in Portugal and now Spain. I must admit that today is the highlight so far for me. I am a ten year convert to the Moslem religion and way of life; a bit difficult in Philadelphia but so be it. I think you have been very fair in your comments on the Moors from long ago and to our religion and culture in general, but I wonder if I might make a modest suggestion, er, that is, if you are open to it."

"Faisal, absolutely. Go ahead."

"I think (I have read your biographic details from the trip brochure, and have listened with great pleasure to all your talks) it is most amazing that you as a farm boy from Nebraska have been inclined to and made a life of teaching other peoples' cultures, in this case Catholic Spain and Portugal and their dominions, especially Brazil. My point, as important as the Moors were (800 years!), what do you actually know of their culture and by the way have you read "The Koran?"

"Lamentably Faisal, no. I do know superficially the accomplishments of Moorish civilization in the Peninsula – edifices, architecture, blue – tile decoration, and the fact they rescued much of Classic Greek Culture and brought it to Europe, along with great strides in medicine, agriculture and mathematics, some of which we'll see in Granada. That's about it."

"Mike I would just urge you to do us Muslims the courtesy to at least read a condensed version of the Koran. We are the second largest religion in the entire world, after your Catholicism, with almost one billion adherents. Our beliefs are simple: There is one God; Muhammed is his 'perfect messenger' and is the last prophet. Our ritual prayer is also simple: pray five times a day facing Mecca, Muhammed's birthplace in 570 AD."

"Faisal, I know little of the details of your faith, but I do know examples of its system of justice, the extreme punishments, and in our own realm here in Spain, the second wave of Muslim advance in Spain by the Almoravids' Yusuf ibn Tashufin was led by a ruthless, bloodthirsty Berber barbarian. And finally, Muslim expansion was by the sword. Christ preached peace and love your neighbor."

"The story is a lot more complicated than that and my friend you might recall the so – called 'Christian Crusades.' Was that not defending the faith by the sword? And the edicts expelling good people from Spain and then accusing them of heresy and false conversion by the Inquisition?"

"Faisal, this is getting us nowhere. There were abuses on both parts, but way too complex for us either to recall or decide. I do encourage you to continue your faith and especially your admiration for Averroes to come soon, almost as we speak "

"So be it. Allah be praised. If we all could have these discussions, life would be much improved. I look forward to Averroes. Peace to you my friend; I'm glad we had the conversation. I hope I've planted a seed. The Koran. Our Holy Book."

AVERROES AND THEN THE JEWISH QUARTER OF CÓRDOBA

Faisal should be happy. After the Mosque we went to the quarter where we saw the statue of Averroes, Córdoba's greatest Muslim intellectual. The biography blew me away: he wrote of philosophy, theology, medicine, astronomy, physics, psychology, and mathematics. What am I leaving out? Of greatest fame was his study, admiration, translation and commentary of the works of the Greek Philospher Aristotle, for this receiving the title of "Commentator" by the Christians. This is what they mean when they say the Arabs were responsible for the recovery and development of Greek Philosophy in the West (much abandoned in Christian Europe after the fall of the Roman Empire). Thank you, Averroes.

Maimónides, Córdoba

And of equal importance was the move on to the old Jewish quarter and the statue of Maimonides. He was a contemporary of Averroes in the

12th century in Córdoba. Intellectual, philosopher, writer, he became best known for his commentary on Jewish Scripture, and an expert on the Torah and wrote his own "13 Principals of the Faith," the required beliefs of Judaism. What we saw in Córdoba was proof of that great age of relative tolerance by Muslim rulers, and an intellectual "renaissance" of the three faiths, Moslem, Jewish and Christian (meaning the Christians living under the Moors, called "Mozárabes," long before the Spanish crown would defeat the Moors in Al-Andalus at the end in 1492).

There was one remaining synagogue in Córdoba. It was beautiful with ornate stucco in the Arabic "mudéjar" style. Done in 1315, it may have been a private synagogue by a businessman or a trade guild's religious place. They don't know for sure. But something is better than nothing. Adventurers admired it; I noticed Rachel deep in thought and who knows what memories and prayers. Amy and I both were moved to see it. Our final and most important one would be later in Toledo.

So, what a memorable day. For all of us. I just add a Spanish major footnote: Spain's Golden Age Baroque poet, Luís de Góngora, "el príncipe de las tinieblas," ["the prince of darkness"] was born in Córdoba and lived there before fame and fortune took him to Madrid, the new capital.

AT and Amy outdid themselves at our lodging that night – Córdoba's "Parador" just the first of many on our "gira." These five – star hotels, often new, but built on historic ruins, or yet modified castles, were the crème de la crème for Spain (and Portugal with their version called "Pousadas," but this was our first chance). We had late afternoon to walk the grounds, enjoy the great swimming pool and a cordoban dinner that evening. Dinner was the local version of gazpacho, grilled meat with all the sides and the local cordoban speciality of wine – the Montillas – but cuidado! A very high alcohol content. The locals say they are much better than the famed sherries of Cádiz. A few adventurers inadvertently tested the theories. Not a wine drinker per se myself, I learned I had to be careful. Let's say this – it loosened everyone's tongue. Including Harry's who admitted that his Port was the best for after dinner, but these were great accompaniments for the fine food.

There were thanks from Faisal saying this was a first great step in his seeing the Muslim heritage, from Rachel who thanked us for the stop at the Synagogue (it wasn't on the schedule) and others. However, it was that newcomer, Sophia Pagello, she of the Roman bridge, who drew most attention. She was, incidentally, seated next to Father David and they seemed to have a lively conversation. It was then, inadvertently, that we learned she was nobility, a Countess from no less than the long line of the Medicis in Florence. She blushed when Harry introduced her as "Countess Pagello," saying, "We in Florence are proud of all this, but today there are dozens if not hundreds of 'old nobilities' in Italy, and I'm not sure anyone can keep up with the sons, some illegitimate, of nobility in the Curia!" Laughter but no denials; their fame precedes them. "Just call me Sophia." I still sensed an undercurrent of what can I say, sadness, melancholy? But the food and wine, loud talking and laughter of others overshadowed that brief interior observation.

I did get to go on some about that Cordoban poet Luís de Góngora and how I needed an entire table in the Georgetown Library to prepare for class. You had to have the text, a very good Spanish dictionary, ditto a Spanish – English dictionary, a dictionary of literary terms, but most of all a dictionary of "Gongorismos," the tropes he used to make the poetry at least in the minds of many, almost indecipherable. "But was it worth it? (said Harry)." "I do not know, but I earned an A and I'll never forget him. I'm sure, Harry, he would not dare be compared to Shakespeare." "Indeed, but old Will had his dark moments as well, and some tens of thousands of lines by critics trying to figure him out. I avoided most of that by reading Theology. Oh, I forgot, it seems to have its conundrums as well." Laughter.

This was *one* romantic place! The proof being Amy and my stroll in those gardens after dinner and a "business meeting" in her room later. We got reacquainted and both raved a bit about the day's activities. She did mention both Rachel (again) and Sophia and wondered how I liked them (innocent question?) "They're okay." Hmm. We talked of the next day, could Granada and the Alhambra top this? Soon to see.

15

GRANADA

Early next morning adventurers were off in the coaches for travel to Granada and the Alhambra. On my coach I was given the microphone and chose to add a literary note and then a general introduction to Granada. What we would see cannot be separated from the literature associated with the area.

"We are not in Gaherty's Spanish Literature class! I already talked of Luis de Góngora, 1561-1622 in Córdoba, but there is much more.

"El Duque de Rivas, 1791-1865, was one of the most famous of the Spanish Romanticists. His play 'Don Álvaro o la fuerza del sino' ['Don Álvaro or the Force of Destiny'] is one of the masterpieces of the Romantic period and was of course later adapted by the Italians to a famous opera 'La Forza del Destino.' He was born in Córdoba, studied at Cádiz and later played a major role in the Liberal Cortes of 1814. Then along with other liberals he was exiled in France and returned to Madrid in later years.

"Federico Garcia Lorca was born in Fuentevaqueros a small town outside of Granada. He was a student and poet at the famous 'Residencia de Estudiantes' in Madrid, later traveled performing folk drama through Spain (there is a real parallel in Brazil with Ariano Suassuna and colleagues' 'Teatro do Estudante de Pernambuco' when they set as a goal the performance of theater for the masses in the tiny plazas of northeastern Brazil in the 1950s), ventured to New York City to write some wild verse, and then returned to Spain only to face death in 1936. Legend has it, but contested, his death was attributed directly to the Falange of Francisco Franco. But his gypsy, flamenco flavored poetry has no equal in Spain. I taught and re-taught his poem 'Romance Sonámbulo' last year in the Spanish Literature survey course back in Lincoln."

The coaches passed through rolling hills and low mountains with cork and olive trees and lots of wheat into Granada. It was a very impressive and large bustling city. There are two rivers in the valley, so farming and orchards are healthy, including many orange groves.

"The city is built on a 'vega' or plain with three hills surrounding it with the Sierra Nevada to the southeast with one peak above 11,000 feet which the tourist brochures say has snow year around. The three hills surrounding the city of Granada are the Albaicín, Sacramonte with the gypsy caves and la Alhambra itself. Granada was a provincial capital when Córdoba was the seat of the Moorish Caliphate and was the capital of the 'Almorávides' kingdom which overran the city of Granada in the 11th century. Granada, in turn, reached its full glory with the 'Nasrides' kingdom from the 13th to the 15th centuries. In the latter times the Moorish rulers paid tribute to the Spanish kings of Navarra, León and Castile to leave them alone. Córdoba's nobility had fled and migrated to Granada when Catholic Spain took Córdoba in the 13th century.

"The Nasrides ruled in the 13th, 14th and 15th centuries, but quarreled in the 15th under the Spanish threat. The Alhambra itself was built in the 14th century.

"Legend or fact this is the tale they tell: The Caliph of Granada was in love with a Christian girl, this in the 15th century. His mother the queen fled with him from Granada; they later returned and deposed the king his father and thus put the son on the throne. There were quarrels amongst the Nasrides and a massacre at Abencerrajes by the Moorish rivals during this period. Then the Spanish King Fernando de Aragón seized the boy king. The Catholic Kings arrived in 1492, and the boy king Boabdil and the mother queen handed over the city and went into exile. Thus, the saying arose, 'Weep like a woman over what you could not defend as a man.'

As we rolled into the city, there could only be one first stop – the famous Alhambra Palace. The following are my notes.

THE ALHAMBRA

One Moorish king destroyed the palace of his predecessors and then built his own palace upon the ruins, using the rubble and rocks for the new walls. Interior decoration was most important with all the rooms facing interior patios. The exterior walls were excessively plain. The interior décor is in fact stuccowork – finely modeled plaster in intricate patterns with low relief to catch the light and with built up layers akin to stalactites. The effect is called the "mocárabes." There are ceramic tiles on most interior walls, the "azulejos."

One enters the complex through the Pomegranate Gate built by Carlos V, Hapsburg King of Spain, after the fall of Granada. To one side is the "Alcazaba" the military part. To the other side is the "Alcázar" or palace from the 14th century; this was in effect the "Casa Real" of the Nasrides.

One enters the palace through the "Mexuar," the former council chamber transformed into a chapel by the Spaniards after 1492. From there one has a wonderful view of the Albaicín quarter. One then can see the Mexuar Court with the pool. Then one sees the "Corte de los Arrayanes" (Mrytles) colonnaded at each end with the pool in the center

Another famous room is the Hall of the Ambassadors. This was the audience chamber of the Moorish Kings. It faced the throne. It was domed with cedar wood in a "Mudéjar" ceiling with paneled horseshoe arches and windows on three sides. Ceilings were decorated in stucco and walls with azulejos with more than 150 patterns in this room alone.

Salon of the Two Sisters, the Alhambra

My favorite was the Salon of the Two Sisters for the mocárabes and the blue tiles. Astounding.

The Patio of the Leones, the Alhambra

The "Patio de los Leones" was done in the 14th century by Mohammed V and is in the heart of the palace. There are delicate, colonnaded arcades surrounded by the fountain and the pool.

THE "GENERALIFE"

This complex is connected to the Alhambra palace by a serious of patios and corridors. In the exterior of the Alhambra there are gardens leading to baths – the gardens are stepped and were used as though a gemstone, all with gravity flow. This was the summer palace of the kings with its incredible terraced gardens, cypress, irrigation, pools, fountains and a view back to the Alcázar. "Los cipreses" [cypress] and "las adelfas" [flowering oleander] were impressive. One of my colleagues in Lincoln, a poet and student of great poets, told of relaxing in the gardens and perhaps even writing a poem or two! He was forever inspired by the verse of García Lorca and I can just image him sitting quietly by the fountain and reciting

"Romance Sonámbulo" in a dramatic voice. He is certainly the most poetically inspired of all our professors at U. of N.

The Generalife Palace is surrounded by the elongated court. There is the "Patio de la Acequía" or "Canal Court" – beautiful! And there is a "Mirador" which overlooks the city of Granada and the Darío Valley. As Amy and I sat on one of the benches in the court, I said, "More than one marriage proposal has taken place here. I would do it but I already did that last year. Do you want a repeat, Amy?"

"A lady can never tire of that! I still believe our agreement to hold off on everything until the end of this trip is the best bet. But, hey, thanks again. Oh, by the way do you like pomegranates?" Sigh.

As we exited the Alhambra and were herded along with all the other visitors, playing in my brain was one of the most beautiful of all Spanish guitar solos, "Recuerdos de la Alhambra" by Isaac Albéniz. It's all done in tremolo, is terrifically difficult, but I could actually do a facsimile when in practice. Okay, time to move on to another important place.

THE PALACE OF CARLOS V IN GRANADA

It was started in 1526 and was to be financed by a tax on the Moors. There was an uprising in 1568 which stopped construction. It is purely Classical in architecture, a good example of Renaissance art and architecture in Spain. It was done by Pedro Machuca who studied under Miguel Ángelo. One of its traits is huge, circular patio within the square building. Then …

THE ROYAL CHAPEL ["LA CAPILLA REAL"]

It was begun by the architect Egas in 1506 and was completed by Carlos V in 1526 in part based on the decision of the Catholic Kings ["Los Reyes Católicos"] to be buried at the site of the final "Reconquista" and not at

Toledo which was their main residence at the time. It is in Isabelline style with ribbed vaulting and coats of arms of the monarchs of the Trastamara linage: a single Águila (not the double eagle of the Hapsburgs). A screen is placed in front of the chapel thus providing "rejas;" inside is the mausoleum of the Catholic Kings, the first design from 1517 in Genoa, the second in 1519-20 by a Spaniard. The sarcophagi are all below in the crypt. Isabella la Católica's personal art collection and her crown as well and Fernando's sword are in an adjoining room.

Whew! Enough already. Adventurers were given free time the rest of that late afternoon before all heading to the Parador of Granada nestled within the grounds of the Alhambra complex. This was AT's and Amy's greatest coup so far! It was a former monastery built by Carlos V on the grounds of the old Nasrid Palace. What a pedigree! We all knew AT wanted only the best, and Amy told me later this was the most difficult she had to negotiate up to that point in all her time with AT! I believe it. The actual hotel is in the gardens of the Alhambra, inside the walls. They boast it is the most requested of all 93 Paradores in Spain. I can see why. Kings, Queens, Presidents, diplomats and luminaries stay there. And now adventurers! Amy took one look at the menu and pronounced it Granada "fine dining." Adventurers agreed, but my stomach did not. But the views out the room windows to the Alhambra gardens and from the terrace to the Albaicín Hill beyond were unforgettable.

For the Christians there had been one more sight – the "overembellished" baroque monastery of the Carthusians on the outskirts of town. First time I've mentioned them, but do so because of Harry's comments at dinner:

"These monks go way back, to the 11th century and Grenoble in Switzerland and good ole' St. Bruno. But we in England have a rather sinister note to add: the monks in London during King Henry VIII's time enjoyed great public respect. The problem was Henry wanted them to lead the way and acquiesce to his 'divorce' or perhaps 'annulment' of his marriage to Catherine of Aragon. When they did not, someone ordered a grizzly slaughter of eighteen monks. As you know, Henry got his way anyway with Ann Boleyn, founded the Church of England and proceeded to 'milk' the old monasteries of their land, buildings and wealth. The good news is he maintained some 'faithful' ('converted' clergy) and they took over the best sites. 'Tommy' Cromwell assisted in the legal maneuvers."

Tomorrow it's off to the final leg of out Andalusian 'gira' to the grandeur of pre and post conquest Spanish Andalusia. We're not finished yet!

16

ON TO SEVILLA

The coaches during the several hour ride passed through more of that rich agricultural Andalusian countryside – immense olive groves and sunflower farms (but not the small "pest" of a plant the farmers hated in Nebraska and weeded them out with machete length knives, one of my duties back on the farm). There were many orchards and in fact we drove by one of the famous bull raising centers (we would call it a ranch back home). Our lodging would be yet another Parador, this time built in a real fortress, that of Carmona, just 15 miles outside the immense hustle and bustle (and noise and thieves on motorbikes) of Sevilla.

It seems one Parador tries to outdo the other; none can top that of Granada, but this place had an amazing view over the plain to Sevilla and was perched on a hill for its past military purposes. It indeed was originally a 14th century Arab fortress, looking like one high up on the hill, but now a hotel. They restored walls, turrets, and huge indoor patios to give it atmosphere. We checked in, had a late Spanish breakfast and then climbed up the steps in the coaches to Sevilla; no parking is ever available so we had to be on our toes for pick up times designated by the guides. Here are my usual notes for this amazing place.

MIKE'S INTRODUCTION TO SEVILLA - CAPITAL OF "ANDALUCÍA"

Hey, adventurers, we have a precedent! Another cultural, literary note before more serious matters: the great Romantic poet Gustavo Adolfo Bécquer was born here before aspiring to and then living life in Madrid. He was known for his book "Rimas" ["Rhymes"] in the 19th century. The straight forward verse is among my favorites in Spanish poetry.

The "Torre de Oro" on the Guadalquivir was built in 1220 to guard the port; it had a chain hooked to the other side of the river to stop boats from passing upriver.

Sevilla was already converted to Christianity when the Alhambra was being built, but chose to maintain the "Mudéjar" style. It was originally an Iberian town, later a Roman capital until it was replaced by Toledo in 711 with the conquest by the Arabs. When Córdoba fell to the Almóhades, Sevilla was made a Moorish capital from 1184-1197. The Almóhades king defeated the Christians in 1195 and he built the Giralda Tower; originally it was a minaret. In 1248 King Fernando III of Castile defeats the Moors.

In 1492 Cristóbal Colón sets out on the voyage to what would become "the New World" from Sevilla. Note that Américo Vespucci, 1451-1512, wanted to prove what Columbus had discovered was not the East Indies or its islands but a new continent. Also, a bit later came the Portuguese's Magalhães' voyage around the world in 1519.The sole survivor, one of his captains, was Juan Elcano who returned in 1521.

In 1503 Isabella la Católica had created the "Casa de Contratación" ["The House of Contracts"] in Sevilla to maximize control of the Indies. The records from those times are in the "Archivo de Indias" ["Archives of the Indies"] in Sevilla. Sevilla remained the main port until 1717 when the river silted up and the monopoly passed to Cádiz. A modern historic note: in 1936 the Falange and the "Nacionalistas" led by Francisco Franco started their revolt here in Sevilla.

La Giralda, Sevilla

The buses dropped us on in the plaza in front of the Cathedral of Sevilla with the Moorish Mosque "La Giralda" to the side. We repeatedly warned adventurers of the pickpockets in this city, many operating from ubiquitous motor bikes. The ladies were told to use handbags with two shoulder straps, one across each shoulder in an X. It turned out to be good advice when Mrs. Singh of India had a fright and a spill when one strap was slashed. The "guardia civil" was right there, she was revived by a cold glass of water and continued the tour of the church.

I'm sorry but can't help a tourist aside from my short time in Colombia and warnings from my host: "Never wear an exposed wristwatch here in Bogotá. And all motorists are told to never lower the driver's window or rest their arm on the window. There are cases when thieves zoom by on motorbikes, slash the arm and snatch the watch. Another trick is for one thief to tap on the right hand window when the vehicle is stopped for a traffic light and his accomplice on the other side of the car tears off the watch on the left arm of the driver. Maybe this is why pedestrians in Bogotá mostly wear the woolen "ruanas" over dresses or business suits on the streets. Tourism anyone?

"La Giralda" was begun in the 12th century as a minaret for the Arabs. The top was only completed in the 16th century. It is brick, stone and mortar and even from a cursory glance maintains the Moorish style (but Spanish "Renascentista" on top). It is 230 feet to the top; there are 35 levels of gradual incline. There is a legend that says that Isabella la Católica would ride her horse to the top for the view. Most adventurers made the ever-ascending climb, some huffing and puffing, but it was worth it for the view alone over most of the old historic center of Sevilla and the Plaza de España in the distance. My take: it would be one helluva go kart ride down, that is, if they allowed go karts. Amy wondered if that was a proper scholarly remark. Okay, I apologize. Dirt track memories at the Lincoln County Fair got the best of me.

"LA CATEDRAL DE SEVILLA"

The edifice is massive, thus conjuring the old saying: "We will build a cathedral so immense they will call us madmen." It is third in size of all of Europe, after St. Paul's in London and St. Peter's in Rome. It surpassed in size the Hagia Sofia in Constantinople in 1500 something and is known as the largest Gothic Cathedral in Europe. It is 184 feet high on the inside, has a Gothic and Renaissance exterior, with interior columns and vaulting. Now adventurers with some sense of perspective could immediately recall the portal of Batalha in Portugal, but like everything else in the building, this was "bigger and better" according to Sevillanos and even most Spaniards.

Catafalque of Christopher Columbus, Sevilla

For so many of the adventurers from the U.S. or Latin America we were caught off guard by the bigger than life catafalque where the four kings of Castille, Navarre, Aragón and León carried what is presumed to be the remains of Christopher Columbus. Whether Columbus is still there is quite another matter. Santo Domingo in the Dominican Republic and Havana in Cuba as well as Sevilla claim him. The word is that after Cuban Independence the remains were transferred to Spain. No matter, the monument is impressive.

We have already seen the huge silver monstrance of the Cathedral of Málaga on the occasion of the Corpus Christi Procession. This one in Seville tops it in appearance and probably value. Should one of the curious readers of this account not be Catholic, likely me thinks, that is, if there is a reader, a short non-academic explanation might be in order. In Roman Catholic liturgy, the exposition of the Blessed Sacrament, the Sacred Host which Catholics believe to be the very body of Jesus Christ, in an appropriate "home" or "housing" became essential during the Benediction Services, particularly during Lent. The "home" is known as a monstrance. If you follow the logic, Christ must be placed in the finest, the most elegant, the richest of "homes" (in effect the home away from home – the accepted resting place in the churches is called the Holy Tabernacle. Like the monstrance, it too might be encased in gold.) One can see that non-believers might consider all this as ostentatious particularly when one knew that the gold or silver was mined on the backs of Indian or Black Slaves in the New World. The Liberals of the 19th century finally caught up with all this in excoriating the church in Spain and Latin America and doing their best to separate it from its riches. President Benito Juárez in Mexico, a full blooded Zapotec Indian brought up and cared for when young by the Church is a good example. We have witnessed such finery in the country of Colombia, but locked in bank vaults save for the military guarded Holy Week processions. One might add that a good deal of that same gold from the mines of America was used by the Spanish Crown to pay its debts to bankers and rival nations of Europe.

The main altar or "Retablo Mayor" of Sevilla's Cathedral is Flemish from the late 1400s to early 1500s. It is massive in its intricate carvings in wood, the gold leaf covering them, and with painted scenes, 45 scenes from the life of Christ. (I stopped counting.) The altar piece is the largest of its type in Spain, perhaps in the world, and is impressive for the color and complexity. Amy and I just sat in awe; it was just all "too much." I found myself wondering how anyone, I repeat, anyone, could possibly concentrate on anything when in front of the huge structure. It supposedly took the artist forty years to complete, also in the spirit of "so large they will think we are mad." At dinner later one night ole Mr. Owen of Cleveland piped up, "That church and its gold confirmed all our Protestant beliefs and complaints of the ostentatious Catholic Church, and the reason there are 'no craven images' in most of our churches. It makes me want to swear. Jesus would strike it down, not just for the audacity of the Catholics, but for any sense of justice from the historians who know who mined and suffered and died for all the gold and silver. I note that these same churches have a fixation of telling you the exact number of kilos of each used."

There is no defense or answer other than the short explanation, not defense, I made of the monstrance in the same church. I cornered Mr. Owen and his wife and asked him face to face, "Just out of curiosity, why in the world did you decide to do this trip?" He laughed, laughed some more and said, "I'm going to do a book on what we saw, put every goddamned photo of gold and silver altars and statues I can take in it and take it to my pastor for distribution to all the churches he knows. Other than that, I love AT travel, we've made trips all over the world, like the amenities and atmosphere on the ships, enjoy immensely good food and wine, and love History. It's because Harry is our IAL (and I know he will give us the real 'story' on Portugal and Spain), and I knew you had an open mind to religion in Brazil and Mexico; that is why I signed us up."

"Mr. Owen, even though I am what you call a 'cradle catholic,' have a Catholic University education, did my dissertation on a folk - Catholic phenomenon in Brazil, I can tell you that I could not have gotten through a Rosary, Mass or maybe even an 'Our Father' and 'Hail Mary' before that altarpiece. Too distracting. On the other hand, it is faith that makes monuments whether here, in Jerusalem or Mecca, or in Palenque or the backlands of Brazil. I can only imagine its role in the making of that Cathedral. You might think about that before you finish your book; Martin Luther, Henry VIII, the Protestant leaders in New England, they had faith I believe, just a bit different version of it. We at AT had one of the great cultural anthropologists of the world aboard IA in Brazil back in 1973, and when we witnessed the at times strange and frightening African rituals in Bahia and Recife he said, 'We should never fear this, just be calm and respect it. It is their religion. Their faith.' I've enjoyed the conversation; you've got a lot more of this to experience the next two weeks. I think it's going to be a rather large book." He laughed and we parted amicably.

After that somewhat draining experience in the Cathedral, it was on to the palaces, religious in their own way. First, the Alcázar of Sevilla.

THE ALCÁZAR OF SEVILLA

It is unique in that it was built by a Christian King, Pedro el Cruel, from 1350 to 1369, but all originally in "Mudéjar" style, copying the style of the Alhambra. The Catholic Kings later added on quarters for the personnel of the "Casa de Contratación" the primary bureaucratic entity instituted by Queen Isabella for governing commerce in the New World discovered by Christopher Columbus and conquered by Hernán Cortés, Hernando Pizarro and many others.

Queen Isabella's quarters done in 1504 were modeled on the "Mexuar" of the Alhambra. In architectural terms "If you can't beat 'em, join 'em.!" The newest part is the court of Carlos V, Renaissance style. "La Casa de Carlos V" was built within the complex, but is actually a different building and in the Renaissance style.

As in Córdoba, nearby is the "Barrio Judío" with narrow streets and patios. It is called the "Barrio de Santa Cruz." It reminded of Granada, but alas, with no major synagogue to investigate.

All that we saw and I just told about was reproduced in Sevilla in what they call "La Plaza de España" all done for the World's Fair. Pavillions were constructed to imitate the real thing for the fair and festivities of 1929. Bridges, fountains, and beautiful "azulejos" with scenes from all the provinces of Spain were reproduced. Pardon me, but it made me think of that quirky "Portugal para os Pequenos" we saw in Coimbra along the banks of the river, but as Seville loves to say, "So big they will think we are crazy" or something like that. It was most memorable for the tile scenes of all the provincial capitals of Spain. Wow!

THE FLAMENCO SHOW, SEVILLA

That evening the entire group went to the "Patio Sevillano" for a live flamenco show, our first of the trip. It alternated "cante jondo" with regional dances. We sat in a great spot next to the side of the stage. It was a quite a performance; of particular interest to Mike the amateur classic guitar player who can play four or five "traditional" but ersatz flamenco guitar solos, the guitarist was excellent with "jazzed up" improvised guitar work matched to the "cante jondo" and the voice of two "gitanos" or gypsies. The guitar starts, the "gitano" warms up, then all match the dancers. There was "Zapateado," etc. For those of us familiar with Mexico, the mariachis and the lady dancers, there were comparisons for the stomping of feet. The gypsies won mainly because of the small nails attached to toe and heel of the boots and the ladies' short high heels. The male singers, the "cantaores" were good, I surmise, but I can't help but recall a Brazilian physician's description, "They sing like someone just grabbed their balls." Uh oh, I'll get flack from the flamenco union for that. I understand they yell at each other a lot.

After two exhausting days in Sevilla, the coaches returned us to "home" – the "International Adventurer." Amy expressed relief that all had gone well, her preparations, reservations and the rest. But she said the next two days might be worse – the arrival to Valencia, a morning tour, and then the Spanish rail trip to Madrid and settling in. The Prado and the National Palace in a full day and then the one – day trip to Toledo. Then AT's northern 'gira' will begin, rather long and taxing especially for Amy. I'll give introductory talks along the way. (Ávila, Salamanca, León, Burgos, Aspeitia, Zaragoza and final to Barcelona).

A small moment not noticed by adventurers took place on deck shortly after Málaga. Sophia Pagello was sitting alone on one of the benches facing shore, apparently distraught and dabbing at her face with a hanky. David Siquciros happened to be doing his "constitutional" not in clerical blacks but with breviary in hand when he saw her. He debated for a moment, but decided that being the good Samaritan he has been his whole life, he should at least stop and inquire as to her wellbeing.

"Countess, er, Sophia, I hope I am not intruding, but I think perhaps you are in discomfort. I just wondered if there is anything I can do?"

"Father David, or David, I'm afraid you caught me at a weak moment. Please continue your walk; I'll be all right in a little while."

"Are you sure? Sophia, you know I am a Jesuit priest, and with now ten years' experience, enough to know that a confession, or just a talk can sometimes work miracles (small m). I have plenty of time, no duties unless you count Mike's talk at 11:00 but that's not for an hour. We can't go to my room or yours, but Captain Tony has allowed me since Lisbon to use a small room off the library for consultations. IA does not carry a religious counselor on staff, and he being Portuguese and Catholic, was delighted and it was he who made the suggestion for "possible counseling on board." I can go ahead, make sure no other people are in sight, and meet you there in ten minutes. What do you say? If anyone should accidentally see you, it will be a confession, and all know that is confidential and also not unusual."

Sophia, looked at him, thought for a moment, and said, "All right. I'll see you upstairs in ten minutes. Everyone knows that even Countesses, especially Italian countesses, have need of spiritual consoling."

David said, "Give me ten minutes to go upstairs, secure the room and perhaps be a lookout. Then you come, it is at the beginning of the aisle after the stairway and marked "Private." I will be discreetly seated in a chair in the library lounge and direct you to the room. Don't worry. It will all turn out all right."

It went as planned, David checked to see the room was free, sat down in the closest lounge chair, and minutes later when Sophia walked down the hall, waved to her and let her in the room. He followed, picked up the "Do Not Disturb. Ship business meeting" and placed it on the outside door knob. It was a pleasant room, a little like that of the balcony suites, with a divan, two easy chairs, a large desk and a large sliding door out to a balcony. There of course was no walkway outside, so complete privacy was guaranteed. There was a small refrigerator and David found bottles of water for both of them. He said, "Sophia, should I put on my purple stole? Is this confession or counseling?"

"Perhaps both. (He put on the stole.)

"If that is the case, how long has it been since your last confession?"

"Over a year Father. I guess my only sin can be that of anger, and is self-pity a sin? For two months I have been shutting everyone out of my life and it has become unbearable."

"Anger is a very common human response and is no sin. Now, what you do as a result of the anger, that's another matter. And it is also a very human feeling to feel pity. Anyone harmed by others or events feels it, but of course to varying degrees. And once again, it is what the individual does in response that may create a more serious situation."

"Father, I think you just need to absolve me for being, pardon my language, a "bitch" to my family and friends. The rest I think is a massive need of therapy."

"All right, … "Et Ego te absolvo a peccatis tuis." Your sins are forgiven. Go and sin no more."

David took off the stole; they sat quietly for some time and then he said, "All right, now I am listening as just a friend. You know you can trust me and confide in me, and I think I can be of help. I know words do not necessarily alleviate actions, but I am confident you will feel better just releasing some of that tension of the last 14 months."

"Father David, two years ago I was among the happiest of women on the face of earth. I had met, courted and become engaged to Tomasso Lamborghini. Coming from India that name may mean nothing to you, but in Italy it means everything. He is the son of one of the major owners of Fiat the largest automobile manufacturer in Italy and will inherit one of its largest fortunes. Their prize creation, the Lamborghinis and the name are no accidents. That name is also noble, going back five hundred years to Rome. Tomasso is two years older than I, incredibly handsome, intelligent, kind and with the manner of not only Italian upper-class businessmen but nobility as well. And with a graduate degree in economics from the School of Economics in London; you can't do better than that.

"You can imagine, my family totally approved. Joining minor nobility of Florence with Fiat is reminiscent of old habits – nobility marries nobility often for the family's sake. The wedding was set for Florence in the Duomo for two months ago, and a reception thereafter in a grand palazzo. After that, two days later, a second reception in Rome with photo – shoots in front of the Coliseum, me in a several thousand-dollar white gown, he in formal black, and a Rolls – Royce waiting at the curb. 'The Coliseum business' is a tradition in Rome; you have to grease a lot of palms in city government to get the permission, then hire traffic and local guards to assure there are no problems. The local Roman tourists know this and the paparazzi do too, thus the guards. Well, no need to go on with that; it never happened.

"It all unraveled when a month before the wedding I received an anonymous phone call. The woman said, 'I know your Tomasso quite well, perhaps better than you, and so do two of my friends. I am calling you in the spirit of what we all have in common – being young women and with our honor at stake. I can understand why you may not trust me or even talk to me, but I assure you I am not playing the part of the 'scorned woman' but rather of someone wanting to head off problems for you now and later. You will be receiving shortly a packet delivered to your door by a secure private company; it will be delivered to you with no return address but typed or printed on the cover, 'Love and Honor.'

"The phone line went silent; she hung up. I thought at first, aha, just a jealous former girlfriend, but then the packet arrived at our palazzo the next day. David, photos do not lie. You need not know all they contained, but we use the word "salacious." Damning photos of my Tommaso naked and having sex with not one but three different women, and I had even heard of them and recognized them. His past was no secret to anyone who kept up with the news. I cannot tell you all the emotions I experienced, anger, disbelief (Just trysts? Nothing serious?), shame, and more anger. You know we Italians are famous for our emotions and our tempers. What to do? My mother her me sobbing in my room, saw the photos on the bed, surmised it all, and just held me."

"Mia figlia Sophia, it is most difficult to see this, but I do not doubt its veracity. Tommaso and his entire family have a history. Your father and I hoped that *this time* the young man would rise above all that. It was such an honor for our family and such joy for you."

"Leave me alone Mamá, just leave me alone. Perhaps we can talk later."

"That next day Tommaso called me as usual and came over to the house, all prepared to take me out to a fine dining room in Florence and talk of wedding preparations. I confronted him in the car on the way to the restaurant, sobbing and shaking. He pulled over in one of the piazzas, put his arm around me and asked me why I was so distraught. I pulled the photos out of my handbag and showed them to him. Silence. For a while. He said, 'I can't deny this, but it's in the past. I did not ask any of them to marry me. Can you forgive my past and take me as I am, loving you?'"

"No Tommaso. I have something those women no longer have, their honor and incidentally my maidenhood. I was saving it for you. Just turn around and take me back home."

"He might have refused and done worse, striking me or whatever. There indeed was sorrow in his eyes when he let me out of the car. But there is no going back. I knew it was over and so did he. My parents did try to console me offering to take me on this trip as a distraction and to come with me. I knew their presence would solve nothing, but decided to go ahead and travel. So David, here I am, two more weeks in Spain and then home to … that. It was all kept out of the newspapers, both our families agreeing to just say the 'novios' had thought better and called it off. The press would get that; this was not Tommaso's first such time around, but it was for me. These past three weeks have been a distraction, but there have been a lot of tears at night in my room. I ask myself if I did the right thing, would he indeed have been a good and faithful husband? Would I have ever forgotten the photos? (They stayed in his car; I don't have them.) Many preparations and a lot of money had been spent, now all to no avail. There have always been suitors, and I can only hope and pray someone truly good will show up."

Sophia broke into tears again. Father David moved over next to her on the divan, and just held her. That was when she turned to him, said thank you and gave him a long kiss on the lips. So surprised and taken aback, David, the celibate priest of years, admitted it did things to him and his entire body. He gently just held her, and they both got up.

"How can you ever forgive me, I'm so sorry, it was the moment."

"To the contrary Sophia, thank you. I've always wondered about my manhood and if I made the right decision to go so young to the seminary. You have inadvertently made me feel so much better. Thank you again. I hope I have helped you as well."

"More than you will ever know. I hope we can talk more the next two weeks, but I think you will understand if we wait on that for a few days."

"That indeed is probably for the best. I'll check the hallway and see you safely out, for your own privacy."

It was eleven o'clock that morning, IA was in calm seas on a beautiful day, and I had one hour to introduce adventurers to our next spots on the itinerary. Amy followed with the nuts of bolts of travel and lodging accommodations.

"Ladies and gentlemen, we will be pulling into Valencia harbor in just two hours where we will all disembark and catch the train to Madrid. There will be those who criticize us for just passing through Valencia, but truly, we believe just seeing the huge port and the city as we pass through will have to do. This is the fifth largest container port in Europe and the first in the Mediterranean so you might want to get your cameras out as we dock. All say it is one of the fastest growing cities in Spain, and it is, but you may not know that historically it is part of Catalonia and the first language is 'Catalán.' But like the 'patria chica' people all over Spain, they all it 'valenciano' here. More citizens speak Spanish out of necessity (particularly since the Civil War during Franco's long reign when he mandated that both Valencia and its big sister Barcelona speak only Castilian). There is one huge historical note: Valencia was conquered *from* the Moors by no less than El Cid Campeador at the end of the 11th century and the Cid died there after a subsequent battle when Moors retook the city. They ruled for two hundred more years! Valencia was pounded by the Axis during the Spanish Civil War, persecuted by Franco later (because of separatists and the remains of the anarcho – sindicalist movement and Republicans) and has only recently began its cultural recovery. You speak "valenciano" (related to Catalán) again in the streets, commerce is booming and the port is the proof.

"Amy, what should we all know?"

"Miguel, we will dock at two p.m. and be on the Valencia – Madrid train at 4:00; it still takes five hours to Madrid, but we will pass through Cuenca and you will get to see the town on the cliffs from your seats. Dining and bar service are available. We'll arrive at Atocha Station in Madrid (hold on to your hats and your valuables) which is overwhelming at first sight. But AT has lodging for us at the Ritz (sorry about all that comfort) because Paradores are an hour or two outside the city and in this case, you will be within walking distance of more than you ever dreamed of in Madrid. The Prado awaits us tomorrow in the morning, the National Museum in the p.m. Then time for shopping for Lladró ceramics, a visit to "Las Cuevas" and Madrid's main Plaza, la Plaza de Alcalá, and fine dining before you collapse tomorrow night at the Ritz. For those of you who are newcomers you will find Madrid overwhelming, but beautiful. Our guides plus Mike and Harry will get you through it. As promised in our brochure and itinerary, in two days we will leave Madrid on a long 'gira' to central and northern Spain. I have been dealing with travel agencies and AT's local office for weeks to set this up, so cross your fingers! There is no need reminding you how many stops we shall make, you've all read the trip brochures, but let's simply say "a day at a time" and something incredibly new each day. When possible, we will be in 'Paradores' and you will see more castles than you ever dreamed up. Back to Mike."

"Friends, Madrid will take care of itself and your head will be spinning like Don Quixote's after he read the adventures of the knights errant in all those books that drove him, some say, a bit insane. This is a modern city, a huge city, but with a sense of historical preservation. The problem is that for Spain, it is 'young,' only founded in the early 17th century. You will have to trust AT and us: tomorrow we will see its best, but our goal is to see historic Spain as well, and I think you will be glad to get out of the traffic and noise in just two days. One word of advice; please stick with us and the AT vans, and don't try to compare the subway system to New York. I guarantee you will get lost if you do! You'll need good walking shoes, a whole bunch of money or credit cards and a couple of strong coffees to get you on your way tomorrow. Actually, a leisurely buffet in the Ritz before we walk to the Prado!"

17

VALENCIA, SPANISH RAIL ON TO MADRID

The Next Day – Madrid

Don Quixote and Sancho Panza, Madrid

THE PRADO

After that hearty breakfast, we all trooped over to the Prado and after waiting in line for fifteen minutes were inside at 10:15. The plan was a

Spanish lunch at 1:00 p.m. and then vans to the National Palace. So that's three hours of staring at paintings, enough for me. I've never been to the Louvre but Amy has, and she said its apples and oranges; Paris has French and Parisian Art and the best collections of late 19th century and modern 20th century anywhere. Monet, Manet, Matisse, and Picasso (except for one – the huge "Guernica" at the Prado). The Prado has Italian Renaissance, Dutch, and all of Spain's greats, many paintings a result of the almost 200-year rule of the Hapsburgs, thus the connection to the Holy Roman Empire painters. I might add incredible collections of Greek and Roman but in another museum, and yet another, a fine archeological museum of antiquities.

Lladró Ceramic – El Greco

For anyone at all connected with Spain, or teaching Spanish, *this* was the Holy Grail. I of course was interested in the painters contemporary or close to it to Spain's "Siglo de Oro" Literature, i.e. Cervantes and cohorts. So that meant El Greco, Diego Velázquez, Zubarán, or Ribera. We saw them all, each with his own salon or long corridor. Our guide was terrific, biased to be sure, but with good English, and described all the clichés: the elongated forms and teary eyes of El Greco's (indicating his near ecstasy in religious painting), the stark and wonderful realism of Veláquez ("I can only paint what I see, what is real") and of course "Las Meninas" perhaps the painting that has spilled more critics' ink than any other in history. And you begin to understand just a bit the intense Catholicism of Spain with Zubarán and Ribera.

I was struck by the 18th and early 19th with Goya, the tapestries but also the court paintings, the zest ("La Maja Vestida," "La Maja Desnuda") with the scandal of affairs and court matters (our guide went on and on about the love affairs). And his "dark period" perhaps of incipient dementia made us all a little crazy. But after two and one half hours, sore and with tired feet from standing before the masters, Amy and I overheard Mr. Owen from Cleveland say as he stood in the back of the small crowd listening to our guide wax eloquent over "Las Meninas," "I hate this shit." It was extremely difficult to not laugh out loud, but Amy and I had our motto for the next two weeks: anything beautiful or impressive and we would whisper to each other, "I hate this shit." So, buoyed by yet another Spanish coffee, we were escorted to the "Piece de resistance" in the Prado annex - Picasso's "Guernica."

Everyone had heard of this one, mainly due to the Axis's bombing of several cities in Spain, but Guernica in the Basque Country the first and becoming a symbol for all. I personally am not a fan of Cubism (Amy is, but she's got more art sense than I), but the agony of both animals (the bull, the horse) and people hit you right between the eyes. Oops, not a good phrase to use after seeing Picasso's cubist faces. We were contemplating all this when the there was a blast of noise and the sirens suddenly started. Then came orders to clear the building, but not to leave the Prado area. The noise was deafening, but all of the patrons dutifully filed outside to the big patio. News whether rumor or fact came quickly: a bomb had been detonated in the Atocha Metro Station, always jammed with people. And ETA had done it.

ETA (the Basque Separatist Organization from Spain's north) as recently as 1973 had killed Franco's prime minister with a terrorist bomb, and although Franco had died in 1975, matters were still tense between the Basque separatist movement and the new Constitutional Monarchy headed by King Juan Carlos Borbón. For that matter, the Catalonian separatist movement, not nearly as violent, but still clamoring for independence, was also simmering on the burner. AT and adventurers were aware of all this when they signed up for the trip, but things had been quiet, or relatively so, for four years and with good signs of stability and progress.

There were police cordons all around the Prado; instructions were that the business district downtown was locked down. Subway stations obviously closed, but taxis permitted to run. After some negotiation and explanation by our local guides, adventurers were permitted to walk in a group back to the Ritz and stay put until further notice. How can I say this: Madrileños were somewhat used to this, the last big attack in 1973 when ETA killed one of Franco's ministers, an incredibly daring act. The staff at the Ritz at reception, in the bars and later at dinner did not seem to be particularly perturbed. But it did bring a lively discussion in the bar before dinner.

Several of us were seated around tables conversing about our likes and dislikes of paintings in the Prado, but mainly the bomb. I met a new adventurer couple - Ramón and Graciela Madariaga, he a distant relative of the famous historian already mentioned. They live in Charlotte, South Carolina, think the Spanish beaches, so far, are inferior. He is pro − Franco, laments all the strife now in Spain. Franco was "the good old days" when you could walk down the streets at midnight and be safe (a common 'cliché' I think) because of the 'guardia nacional' (the funny hats). Today it's pickpockets, half naked women on the beaches, pornographic magazines in the news kiosks, and marijuana smokers. And pro − abortion protests in the streets.

A couple at the next table heard the remarks and spoke up loudly. It was José and Cecilia Ronda from San Francisco, their opinion the opposite: "Spain is coming out of a dark cloud; if you know any history, Franco's atrocities are innumerable: the slaughter of thousands of Republicans, communists, anarcho – syndicalists and many innocent citizens for starters. One million people died in his war and dictatorship. They are now discovering mass graves all over Spain. And hey, Franco's "peace" didn't exactly work in 1973 when he couldn't even protect his ministers."

Both men stood up and I thought they would come to blows, but calmer voices prevailed, mainly that of Harry who was seated nearby. "Friends, the past is past and even if it is not, we have two more weeks to enjoy this historic and wonderful country. I can't call a meeting but have left written notice at the reception desk; we have a necessary change of plans. We shall travel by coach tomorrow to Toledo and its historic grandeur, and the 'gira' will commence from there. Once again there are still a few adventurers out on the streets, so either the guides or Mike or I will provide you with a prep on Toledo while on the coaches tomorrow morning. Departure at 8:00 a.m. a bit early, but there is much to see. We will have a handout prepared by Amy for you on the coach; needless to say, she's 'on call,' with the lodging changes. To avoid changes of weeks of planning work we may stay one extra day in Toledo."

I was surprised when both men of the Franco dispute shook hands and agreed to table their differences. Whew. We all got to bed enjoying that "old money" atmosphere of the Ritz (and some said later "the old beds and dripping faucets as well"). I ate breakfast with Amy at 7:00 and got her preview of accommodations in Toledo. The good news was she got us into the famous "Parador;" the bad news was because of the late date all rooms were in the back and missing the view of Toledo in front. But, the pool, the huge indoor restaurant, the outdoor restaurant and terraces all had the view, and she cajoled the management to provide free cocktail vouchers (2 each night) for all the adventurers, thinking it might sooth their nerves. And besides, the view to the high plains around Toledo was not too shabby.

The one-page flyer explained most of this and had the view from the hotel in a color photo; we gave them out to all adventurers. I gave the people in my coach an introduction to Toledo and understand Harry did in the same in another.

18

ON TO TOLEDO

MIKE'S INTRO TO TOLEDO - HISTORY AND IMPORTANCE OF TOLEDO

Toledo was founded by the Romans with the Latin name "Toletum" and became the center of the peninsula. After the fall of Rome, it passed to the Visigoths who made it their capital and then abandoned it when the Moors attacked and took over in 711 and incorporated Toledo into the emirate of Córdoba. It would remain with this title until 1012 with the revolt of the Taifas and it was elevated to a new status: capital of an independent Taifa kingdom. It was finally retaken in 1085 by Spanish King Alfonso VI of Castile who two years later moved the Spanish capital from León to Toledo and it had the title "Imperial City."

It was the most important city in all Spain for the Jews who reached a population of 12,000 in the 12th century. Alfono X "El Sabio" established the "School of Translators" in Toledo with Jewish participation which lasted until the pogrom in 1355 by the Trastamara family. There was a later massacre and the final straw was the expulsion of the Jews from Spain in 1492. Prior to that Toledo was known in the Middle Age as a place tolerant to the three cultures of the peninsula: Christian, Jewish and Moslem. We would see two important synagogues, and I had promised Rachel back in Portugal I would be there with her in Toledo. The "Reyes Católicos" Ferdinando and Isabella of the 15th century liked the city and planned to be buried here – there was a change in plans and they ended in Granada.

Other dates (no test, don't worry)

In the 16th century in 1516 Cardinal Cisneros takes over as regent when Ferdinand dies. Carlos I (Carlos V of Spain and the Holy Roman Empire) arrives in 1517, speaking more German than Spanish.

Toledo received the title of "ciudad" and became the seat of the Spanish Empire in the 1530s.

In 1561 Carlos V's son Felipe II decides to move the court to Madrid.

In 1577 El Greco moves to Toledo.

In the 19th century there is decadence in Toledo when Napoleón Bonaparte occupies the city with his troops; there are fires in San Juan de los Reyes and in the Alcázar.

In 1936 there is the siege of Toledo by the Rebels under Generalísimo Francisco Franco and the Falange.

AT'S "GIRA"

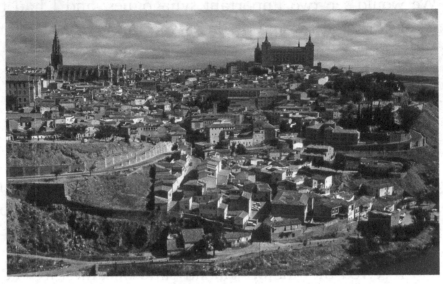

View of Toledo

We were quickly out of Madrid on the four-lane and soon saw brown, rolling hills and wheat. The first view of Toledo is exciting with the view of the Alcázar and the Cathedral from high above. Our coach followed the road up to the site where El Greco painted his famous "View of Toledo." From El Greco's view we also saw the San Martín Bridge, then "La Puerta de Bisagra." All of Toledo in those old days was a walled, fortified city. There are perhaps one-half dozen original entryways to the city. One old restored castle outside the walls was governed by El Cid at one time. Let the expedition begin!

THE ALCÁZAR

We did not visit it, but good to know just the same: it dates from the 13th century, an old military fort, and was reconstructed from the 16th century under Carlos V in 1537. It was set afire by the English and the Portuguese in the 17th century in 1710 in the War of the Spanish Succession (the former supported Archduke Carlos of Austria and lost). It was made into a house of charity, then a military academy. As such it suffered the siege by Franco in the Spanish Civil War in 1936.

THE CATHEDRAL

This would be our main stop and rightfully so. This is the official Apostolic See of Spain yet today; it is one of the great buildings of Spain. Our friend Mr. Owen of Cleveland smiled and said, "Here we go again." In spite of our differences he always managed to be on my coach. Hmm. The Spanish Catholic Cathedral was built on the site of a Visigoth Cathedral and made a mosque by the Arabs in 1000. After the Spanish took Toledo there was construction in 1227 by King Ferdinando el Santo. The nave was roofed only in 1493; it took 266 years to finish. Photos were prohibited and purchased slides were copyrighted. (We did not have that problem in Portugal at all, and the Portuguese let us all know it.) I told adventurers to take pictures of what they could but would have to use their encyclopedias at home for memories and trip diaries. Sorry. But here's the "short list" [ha!] of what's inside.

> The portal of 1337, just one among many, the style reflecting the time of construction, but this one reminded of Batalha in Portugal and of course Sevilla in Spain.

> The bell tower, "la gorda," a bell of seventeen and one-half tons cast in 1755.

> The interior: there are 5 aisles, and it is second in size to that of the Cathedral of Sevilla. I can't even remember all the side chapels and altars, but more than you need. How many times a day can you go to mass, or for that matter, say mass? Once again, like Sevilla. The main altar yes, coming up.

There are 70 stained glass windows in the choir or "coro" in the center of the nave. The largest is the "Rosetón." Along with the Cathedral of Burgos and especially León it's among the top three in Spain.

The "Reja Renacentista" before the Altar Mayor.

The "Retablo Mayor" was done by the Architect Egas for Cardinal Cisneros between 1497 and 1504, "de madera pintada de oro y policromado." I've already spoken and written at length of such Altar Pieces or "Retablos," namely that of Sevilla. This one almost matched it! Not as large as Sevilla, but you get the idea. Once again, we stopped, looked and marveled, but wondered if things got a bit out of hand. I think you close your eyes when you pray.

The carved wood choir and seats and double eagle music stand, German from 1646. The lower seats, fifty of them in all, at the end of the "coro" detail 15th century scenes of battle in Granada. The upper part of the choir with seventy seats was carved by Berreguete in the 16th century. This is terrific and huge, seen before in Málaga, Córdoba and especially Sevilla, but maybe the best … so far. At least, the largest. I knelt down and tried to look at the detail of one or two, but that makes one weary.

The Sacristry: the main claim to fame is that it is replete with paintings by El Greco.

The Treasury or "El Tesoro:"

The highlight is the Monstrance commissioned by Cardinal Cisneros and done by the artist Enrique de Arce, 1517-1524.

They used 37 kilos of gold and it all was the property of Isabella la Católica. There is a newer monstrance from 1594 of 350 pounds of silver with 5,600 pieces, covered with gold – "an offer to the divinity that we most esteem." The gold base is from the 18th century and is Baroque: four angels carry the Holy Sacrament on Corpus Christi. I've already spoken and written at length of such monstrances in Málaga and Sevilla, but this one gets the "premio gordo" [sorry, a reference to the multi-million-dollar lottery prize in Madrid at Christmas Time, a big present for someone].

After the Cathedral there was "rush" time to see the house and museum of El Greco. This house - museum was inaugurated in 1910, like yesterday in Spanish time, and remains one of the main places to see the great painter's works, although we saw many more in the Prado. El Greco, from Crete, trained by the masters in Rome in the "Manierista" style, of course became one of a handful of great painters of Spain's Golden Age. The most famous painting in the "casa-museo" is his "View of Toledo," although there are other copies of it in diverse places. But it was special to see finally the great painting after our initial stop high on the hill overlooking Toledo and seeing the city as he must have as well! The other is the "El Entierro del Conde Orgaz." This latter masterpiece is my favorite because it incorporates "real" life and people with that Catholic vision of heaven. How can I say this? One does grow weary of the predominance of religious paintings of the Golden Age in Spain. I think Literature one – upped them with "El Quixote" and the Picaresque Novels. And Velázquez provided some variety in the Prado.

LA SINAGOGA DE SANTA MARÍA LA BLANCA"

On the outskirts of Toledo, 1180, it is considered the city's oldest and unique in one very important aspect: constructed under the Christian Kingdom of Castille, by Islamic architects for Jewish Use. This represents that same "golden age" of the School of Translators and religious tolerance if not full cooperation.

LA SINAGOGA DEL TRÁNSITO

Sinagoga del Tránsito, Toledo

Rachel Guzmán was our guide here. 1357-1360. Why? The Synagogue was done by Samuel ha-Levi Abulafia, treasurer of the King of Castile Pedro el Cruel. Rachel is a long – time distant descendant!

The word is the King gave his okay to construct the place to make up for a pogrom in 1348. It was originally to be a private place of worship for the Abulafia family. We are fortunate to have it today for it is one outstanding, beautiful building with a great history. Rachel had told me weeks ago of the descendance of her family, way back, to the Sephardi Jews and to the founder's family. She should be so proud! The hall is "Mudéjar" style with 54 arches with marble columns. Serious stucco work makes you remember Córdoba's Mosque and the Alhambra in Granada. The Torah was kept in the arches. There is praise of Pedro who protected and favored the Jews during his reign. And quotations from the Psalms. After the expulsion of the Jews in 1492, in 1494 the building was turned over to the military "Órden de Calatrava" and was used as an oratory to St. Benedict. It survived the Napoleonic War and anti – religious sentiment in Spain throughout the 19th century, but was preserved (some say miraculously) and made into a Sephardi Museum today. Definitely a highlight of Toledo.

I sat with Rachel on one of the benches, not saying anything. Just calmly looking at the beautiful stucco filigree walls, the wooden mudejar beams and the carved columns. I even held her hand. A privilege! Rachel then asked for some quiet, private time. When I told Harry later, he was duly impressed and grateful that AT and IA had such a person as adventurer in this historic place.

I won't say we were rushed, but can I say it all was a blur. Since Spain's stores stay open late, and Toledo is indeed one of the major tourist spots, there was time late that p.m. for adventurers to see any remaining sights, particularly San Juan de los Reyes Monastery where the Catholic Kings were to be buried – uh oh, change of plans, they are in Granada. The edifice was built by the Spanish after they defeated the Portuguese at Toro and was done at the command of Queen Isabella la Católica herself! It was to be modeled on the Church of San Isidoro in León. It was done in the style of the Gothic-Isabelline and is considered to be the finest building done in Spain by the Catholic Kings! Cardinal Cisneros did his novitiate here. We were interested especially by the gargoyles in the cloister, fine examples of the thinking of the time. I was hoping for rain.

Damascene Artisan Work, Toledo

The local artwork and handicrafts were available in the small shops. The famous "damascene" work, gold thread on oxidized black steel. We watched an artisan painstakingly apply his craft.

Talavera Ceramics, Toledo

Then came the Talavera Pottery from the nearby city of Talavera de la Reina. The ceramics go as far back as the times of Felipe II in the late 17th century who used them in the Escorial. And the famous "Talavera" pottery in Mexico takes its name from this place. One could buy a complete set and then pay the very hefty price of shipping it home to the United States. One or two adventurers indeed did this.

And for all of us who remembered Don Quixote's "home - made armor" but recalled the real thing, we saw entire shops full of swords, shields, lances, all made of Toledo Steel. One source notes that Toledo steel was known since 500 B.C. and that it came to the attention of Rome when they encountered Hannibal and his troops using swords of steel from that region. An adaption of the same became standard in the Roman troops, the Toledo short sword. And the Spanish "conquistadores" were famed for their swords made in Toledo, the same said to not be good unless they could bend in half and deal a blow to steel helmets.

My last memory of Toledo was walking through those narrow, winding streets reflecting the reality of medieval Toledo; this is the way it was and still is! It was late afternoon; the light was special. Most of us were in a hurry to get back to the Parador with the good news greeting us – being Sunday and a relatively "slow" day, our reservations were shifted to the front of the Parador with that incredible view of Toledo! The sangria and wines of central Spain flowed readily at dinner either inside or on the terrace, and even old Wonky got his fill of photos the next morning after breakfast and our departure for the northern 'gira.'

But it's good I think to tie up the loose ends for Toledo, so different from Andalucía yet with reminders (the "retablo" in the Cathedral and especially the art of the "Sinagoga del Tránsito"). It had been some time, but for some reason, I was at a table at dinner with our Brazilian and Portuguese friends. Their take on Spain, people, wine and food was informative and a bit hilarious. Amy had joined us after being in the Parador all day on the telephone setting up details for the next three days. The conversation was primarily in Portuguese. What can I say? I had missed it and was a bit rusty. After two or three glasses of "Garnacha," the red grape specialty of the region (unlucky name, we all called it "Gotcha.") Antônio Sarvaiva gave the Portuguese "take" on Spanish or "castellano"), "The Spaniards say speaking Portuguese is like speaking Spanish with mush in your mouth. We say Spanish is like Portuguese but with a speech impediment!" Laughter all around.

19

THE NORTHERN "GIRA"

It will start tomorrow, first a quick stop in Ávila and then two nights in Salamanca. Then Amy has prepared two options since it is a long trip. A is to Burgos, Zaragoza and back to Barcelona for departure. B is a sort of religious 'gira' for those interested: León, Burgos, Aspeitia, and Barcelona.

ÁVILA

Wall of Ávila

On the way to Salamanca we just had time for a short stop in Ávila. This is one of Spain's best examples, among many, of the walled medieval city. Plus, the site of Santa Teresa de Jesus's museum. Adventurers found it a bit bleak, grey and old. It was the coldest, highest spot yet on our 'gira," and the highlight was seeing the ring on her finger in a jar of formaldehyde. Hmm. She is famous for founding "Las Monjas Descalzas," of the Carmelite Order, and her relation as friend and mentor of San Juan de la Cruz who founded the male order of Carmelites. She is considered a possible "mystic" with her "Moradas." He is in the august group evidenced by "Dark Night of the Soul." Some adventurers complained we did not stop in Segovia to see the "Disneyland Castle" and his tomb. Amy and Harry apologized and said, "Maybe next time."

On to Salamanca where I as cultural leader would have a lot to say because once again of the importance of the place to Spanish education and literature.

SALAMANCA

I gave a short introduction on the coach: Salamanca and its History

"It dates from the earliest natives of the Peninsula, 'los Íberos' that is, was later conquered by Hannibal in the 3rd century B.C., and later flourished under the Romans as evidenced by the bridge across the Tormes (Sophia will be happy, another Roman contribution to Spain, 'Another Bridge to Cross.'"). It was invaded several times by the Moors but was taken by the Christians in the Reconquista by Alfonso VI in 1085. Jump seven centuries and it was occupied by the French in 1811 and was freed by the Duke of Wellington in 1812.

The 'Gira' in the City of Salamanca

On our way into the city we saw the professor's first link to the literature of Spain's Golden Age – the bridge over the Río Tormes and its small role in the best of Spanish picaresque novels, "Lazarillo de Tormes." There is a famous scene in the novel when the picaro Lázaro outwits one of his 'amos,' [masters] the blind beggar, by getting him to butt his head against the stone statue of a bull on one side of the bridge, and in the interim Lázaro escapes from his first cruel boss. Some adventurers laughed, "Profe, you are getting a bit esoteric here. More like 'bull – shit' I think." Laughter and protests by me.

Plaza Mayor de Salamanca

After arriving we had a late lunch outside the hotel in the Plaza Mayor, listened to music from the "tunas," that is, the students dressed in gowns and faculty ribbons and singing sometimes ribald university songs, and saw the famous storks or "cigueñas" on the steeples (they migrate from Northern Africa and our adventurer birders were ecstatic). Our hotel was a bit rustic, not quite up to AT standards, but Amy said, "All right, you can't win 'em all. Don't mention this in your final expedition survey." Dinner that first night was in a restaurant in the Plaza Mayor, seafood: "almejas, gambas, langostinos, y cigalas.' Uh oh, I got to tell my Spanish joke on Castilian pronunciation – the "theta" or lisping sound when pronouncing the "c" or z." I kept repeating ad nauseam "Voy a comer cigalas en la Plaza de Zaragoza." Just a few people got it, mainly the Portuguese who loved it, confirming Antônio's theory on language. "Hey, you might get a chance to repeat it when you are having drinks in that plaza." That night it was rainy and cold. The Plaza Mayor viewed through our restaurant windows was almost empty. I slept like a log in spite of incredible street noise. Nebraska students party but not like this.

Tourism the next day due to time constrictions would be divided in two options, either followed by free time ("It's about time" hollered an adventurer) in the afternoon. One had to choose: the church option of the Plaza Mayor, Casa de las Conchas, La Clerecía Church, la Catedral Vieja and the Catedral Nueva, or the University of Salamanca. I would choose of course the latter and along with the guide clue in adventurers to its amazing history and importance.

The University of Salamanca

After a wake – upper of churros and café con leche, the next morning my group was off to the university. Harry was along ("I've seen enough of European churches anyway. I want to see this and evaluate if it really can come up to speed with Oxford," he slyly quipped). I was incredibly excited to be at this place. The University was founded in 1215 (by the way, Harry, Oxford was in 1167 followed by Bologna, so Salamanca was in the "ball park"). It was part of the patronage of the Kings of Castile and was important in the days of the Counter-Reform in the 16th century. We would now see the actual classrooms of writers linked to my Spanish Graduate Studies at Georgetown - the Renaissance - "Mystic" Poet Fray Luis de León, the Renaissance-Golden Age poet Garcilaso de la Vega, and the Iconoclastic Philosopher - Thinker Unamuno as Rector in the 1930s. You have to start somewhere so why not the entrance?

Fray Luis de León and the University of Salamanca

El Patio de la Escuela. The entrance to the Universidad de Salamanca dates from 1534 and was done primarily in the Plateresque style; there are three levels to the entrance, the first from the time of the Reyes Católicos, the second from Carlos V, the third from a Pope What's His Name. Of principal interest on the entryway of carved stone was the symbol of the Hapsburgs – the Spanish double eagle. In front of it is a large statue of Fray Luís de León.

He was one of its main lecturers in the 16th century. Priest, philosopher, theologian, poet and writer, he was condemned by enemies (possibly linked to the Inquisition) for translating to Spanish the Psalms of the Old Testament, a no – no of the times and surely a link to his being related to Jewish "conversos" forced to convert to Catholicism or be expelled from Spain but secretly practicing their old religion. We saw the pulpit from which Fray Luis de León lectured and the carved student benches with student names. (I insisted Wonky take a picture of me from the pulpit, "lecturing as it were" like my literary hero.) His "Vida Retirada" is one of my favorite poems with its theme of getting away from the hustle and bustle of the Spanish Court and leading a simple, pure life in the country.

Remember it is just a poem following literary models of the age. It might be explained by Fray Luís's being locked up in a dreary jail for a time before being allowed to return to his classroom. A legendary quote is in all the literature books, "As I was saying yesterday … ." He is buried in the chapel of the university.

One of his students almost matched his fame, the Golden Age Renaissance poet Garcilaso de la Vega (not to be confused with a writer in colonial Peru with the same name). Garcilaso was the best of poets of his age, refined but classic style; I had an entire semester seminar at Georgetown on him. We searched for but never found his name scratched on the student benches in front of Fray Luís's lecture podium.

And last but not least was the long courtroom – like bench from which the irascible Miguel de Unamuno held forth as a professor of Greek (!) and as Rector of the University in the 20th century prior to fleeing to exile in France from the Franco regime (Unamuno was a notorious Republican and Liberal). Once again, I suffered through an entire semester of Unamuno at Georgetown. That's when I learned the term "idée fixe," an intellectual obsession as it were; Unamuno in his private life fixated on his struggle to maintain his Catholic faith and spent a good deal of his adult life writing about it. We read "Sentimiento Trágico de la Vida" and several of his novels, apropos "San Miguel Bueno Mártir," always the same theme. It did not help my own faith. Okay. But give the Jesuits credit – they did not ignore him!

Suffice to say, all these figures were important to me during my years of graduate study of Spanish Literature at Georgetown and even more when I taught on a regular basis the Survey of Spanish Literature – Golden Age – at the U. of N. This was another highlight of Spain in my relation to studies of Golden Age Spanish literature; Córdoba and its connection to "El Príncipe de la Escuridad," Luis de Góngora, was a close second. Madrid and writers there in the 17th century followed. No sense it leaving out Cervantes, but his place of birth, Alcalá de Henares outside of Madid, is small and never made it on Amy's list.

So that concluded the two – hours at the University. Harry and I would discuss it all later and it was "checkmate" – he had not studied about Salamanca and I had not studied about Oxford. Adventurers probably cared less, but ole' Antônio Saraiva put in his two cents' worth reminding us of Coimbra.

All this conversation took place either at dinner again in Salamanca or on the coaches. The Church group added their reflections, and I would be remiss if I ignored them. As follows:

Salamanca – the New Cathedral 1513-1560.

It is late Gothic and Plateresque with carved stone doorways and the Baroque choir.

Salamanca – the Old Cathedral

It is 12th century Romanesque and old Gothic with an outstanding "retablo" or high altar. The apse with its many compartments was painted in 1445-1453. Very impressive. The Santa Bárbara Chapel was the selected place for university graduate exams. Adventurers chided me for not being along. The candidate would place his feet on the stone feet of the Bishop's tomb and answer questions from the likes of Unamuno. I would have gotten "cold feet."

The Monasterio de San Estéban.

There was a Gothic and Renaissance mixture inside with a Plateresque façade, similar to that of the university. Churriguera (of later fame in Mexico) was the architect and it featured a gold, baroque altar.

One final highlight, almost an accidental discovery, was the Iglesia de San Marcos. The latter was from the 1100s, was round in shape with narrow slits for windows in the thick medieval walls and was "mozárabic" inside. I think this was the oldest Catholic church so far in Spain. Stay tune folks.

Church group people were happy especially with old medieval "retablos" and Romanesque churches. Wonky snuck some pictures and said he would send them to us all. Soon enough.

That night at dinner once again in the Plaza Mayor; I daresay it reminded of the same in Madrid, but this one better for the music and folkloric dances we got to see. There were some sad goodbyes as perhaps two – thirds of the adventurers, admitting to being a bit weary, chose the option to leave for Zaragoza and then departure at Barcelona. Rachel Guzmán was among them; she thanked me profusely and in private said, "If it were not for other circumstances, I think you and I could have much more to say." Hmm. But they were happy campers, grateful for the amazing trip and already asking Harry, me, and Amy what would come next. Who knows, but Amy and I had an idea or two I will tell later. It worked out well with a small group in just one coach for the northern 'gira.' David Siqueiros, Sophia Pagello, all the Portuguese and Brazilians stayed on, good Catholics interested in León and then the Jesuit tradition.

20

LEÓN AND FESTIVITIES

We had to backtrack some to the northwest, but so be it. León is on the "Via de Santiago" and it would have been nice to see it after or in conjunction with Santiago de Compostela, but trip logistics with the ship docked in La Coruña did not allow it then. In a way it related just as well now to our in a sense religious "pilgrimage."

TRAVEL TO LEÓN

The coach continues to León. It was green and pretty until Orense, then rougher country. Galicia in retrospect really agreed with me. David is along, no surprise, all the Portuguese. Mr. Owen of Cleveland had had enough, but he was warm and gracious in his goodbye last night, said if you're ever in Cleveland we'll go to an Indians' game (he and I had talked of my teenage years as a baseball fan and how I knew of all those old Indian pitchers – Bob Feller, Bob Lemon, Herb Score, and even the short-lived Satchel Paige time.)

TOURISM IN LEÓN

Stained Glass, Cathedral of León

We arrived mid – morning, just a two-hour drive from Salamanca, so the tourism began. The guide said the surrounding area was famous for trout streams, but, alas, no time for that. We did a quick check – in at our lodging, the Parador on one side of the main plaza, but then it was the "business" of tourism. First on the list was the Cathedral, ho hum, but for one real reason – the stained glass! Amy, David and others were in my group. All I remember of the guide's comments:

"Originally Gothic, there is a baroque choir, but the real feature is the stained glass, comparable to Rheims, Chartres and the best of French Gothic. 1800 square meters of the same from 13th to 15 centuries!"

We all marveled, remembering Sevilla and Toledo, but these windows topped them all. León along with Burgos (next on the itinerary) and Santiago de Compostela (already seen) are the big three Gothic Cathedrals on the Way of Santiago. There was time before a late Spanish lunch at about 2:00 p.m., more to see, now in the old, historic north of Spain, the really old Romanesque heritage.

THE CHURCH OF SAN ISIDORO

Medieval Monk, San Isidoro, León

It represented the best of the Romanesque with rounded arches and paintings in the original 12th century style. These were unlike any we had seen yet, truly medieval! The paintings seemed primitive indeed. We saw the medieval manuscripts by the monks, the beautiful colored hand – painted illustrations. I understand the Book of Kells in Ireland of all places has comparable things. I think we were all weary, just a half – hour there.

Ah, lunch, it was one of the more memorable on the 'Gira," and one that brought me a reprimand later from Amy. All of our group spent two hours at a local inn near the Parador with local wine, a "claret," served in ceramic jugs. I forget the food for some reason. I must have mistaken the jugs for old, iced tea pitchers on the farm growing up. One does not drink claret in such fashion. Perhaps it was however responsible for one of the times on the trip with the most laughter. We drank (some of us) to excess, I think they all it "juerga" in Spain ["partying to excess"]. Antônio Saraiva and I were inspired to return to the Cathedral, partly his fault saying he wanted to see once again and compare to O Porto similarities, so he and I wobbled off to the Cathedral. By this time well along in the trip, plus the camaraderie at lunch, we were best of friends. Both of us old cradle Catholics and lovers of language, literature and music, we could not help but notice the incredible acoustics of the Cathedral and were moved to recalling our youth at mass and Gregorian Chant. Antônio knew Latin and real Chant; I had a great memory for melody. We commenced to do a duet of sorts, he first in Latin, I then in ersatz made – up Latin (like comedian Sid Caesar on his "Show of Shows" when he did the fake German as an SS officer). There was much laughter and carrying on. But only for maybe five minutes. That was when the sacristan arrived and summarily threw us out of the Cathedral. Chagrinned but not demoralized, we continued the singing on our blurry way back to the Parador, congratulating each other on our performance (Antônio would tell me later it was one of the most memorable moments of his Life!). Amy was seated in that great lobby, saw what shape we were in, and, fuming, marched me ever so subtly to our room. Later on, after my two hours' nap, she had calmed down a bit. Calmer but not forgetting.

"I guess you know this is strictly a no – no for AT staff. But I've seen it before many times on "Adventurer" with the naturalists. You might suggest to your partner in crime that he keep it under his hat, or at least minimize it for adventurer consumption."

"Yes, boss, yes ma'am."

There was repentance and remorse the next a.m. I had a talk with Antônio who really thought nothing of the whole thing, "Reminds me of when I wore the ribbons at Coimbra!" He turned out to be very "cool" about it, and other adventurers just heard that we had a good time in revisiting the Cathedral (but no mention of the Sacristan). Amy concluded, "Gaherty, you owe me one." We managed to have a civil, quiet dinner with other adventurers that night in the Parador, and someone commented I was very quiet.

Entrance, Parador, León

Need I mention, Amy had once again "scored" for AT with this as our lodging. The "Parador" was great with armor, a nice cloister with Roman ruins, antique furniture of 16th and 17th centuries and many paintings.

Santiago Matamoros, León

And of course, a fine image of Santiago Matamoros! One had the feeling of being in a real palace and monastery with three or four floors wrapping around a quadrangle. Or, so I remember.

21

BURGOS AND NORTH TO THE BASQUE COUNTRY

I confess to a nap on the coach the next morning, now on our way to Burgos (to complete the Via de Santiago trilogy). I doubt the stop was too exciting for most adventurers, but for another slice of Spanish history and especially literature, indeed it was. Later, on the rather long coach ride I prepped folks for the place but added the importance for some of the best of Spanish Literature.

"Let's start with the literary history first.

"This is the geographic region for the beginning of the Spanish Epic Poem, 'El Poema del Mío Cid', Rodrigo Díaz de Vivar. I lecture on this at the U. of N. in the Survey of Spanish Literature Course, and I think it is the last you'll hear from me about that. (A voice in the back of the coach said, "Right. Enough already!" But someone else said, "Silence! This is why we are in Spain, come on, Mike, let's get the whole story.")

"Thank you for your respective perspectives. 'El Cid' is important for two reasons: he really did live, was a late medieval paladin in the long odyssey of the early reconquest of Spain from the Moors in the 11th century. The short version is he indeed was at first a mercenary (you had to make a living) for local Moorish leaders, married into the old, old nobility (Doña Ximena) of Castile, defeated an army of the Count of Barcelona and went on to take the important city of Valencia. We all know him from that Hollywood movie with Charlton Heston and Sophia Loren (their version of El Cid and his Spanish wife, incidentally Sophia looks more Italian than Spanish). Our own Sophia spoke up then, "None of you North Americans seemed to mind in the film when she flashed those good looks and figure!" Laughter.

"More important for now, 'El Poema del Cid' is Spain's Epic Poem. Well, yes and no. The thematic national hero with fame and glory (and in his case, lots of money) are there, but the form does not at all follow the 'octava real' of the 'Iliad, Odyssey' or 'Aeneid.' That's what makes it unique – it is written in the original 'romance' rhyme and meter, making it all the more Spanish. Which leads me to part two: Burgos and surrounding area are also the region of a certain part of the old poetic 'Romances' of medieval and early modern Spain. (keep in mind the romances were strong in Andalucía as well; 'Abenámar, Abenámar' etc.) These became for two hundred years *the* main verse, rhyme and meter for 'old Spanish Literature.' Some of the most famous came from the 'Poema del Cid' (or as some argue, existed before and were put together to make the Cid). I'll choose the first theory thank you. The 'Jura en Santa Gadea' ['The Oath in Santa Gadea'] is a case in point: the dramatic challenge of El Cid to King Alfonso VI to swear upon the Bible that he did not kill his own brother Sancho II (who was a patron of the Cid). It makes for good reading. And also for one of the best scenes in the movie which of course took liberties (I won't tell you the last scene when El Cid leaves Valencia Castle for the field of battle.) Oh well, on to the history of Burgos and why I talked about all this.

HISTORY OF BURGOS

"Burgos was founded in 951, the 'Caput Castellae.' It was selected by Fernán González as the capital of the then 'Condado de Castilla.' [This would be the time and place of 'El Cid.']

"In 1037 Fernando I united Castilla, León and Aragón under one kingdom, then battled the Moors to win back Madrid in 1083 and Toledo in 1085. This is the early phase of the famous Spanish 'Reconquista' which would only end in Granada in 1492.

"Real history. 1026-1099. Rodrigo Díaz de Vivar, El Cid, served Sancho II, then Alfonso VI; he was banished for his suspicions of the King and the King's jealousy. He married Ximena, cousin of the King. He served first as a mercenary for the Moorish King of Saragossa. He captured Valencia in 1094, using Moorish troops. He was later defeated by the Moors at Cuenca and died in 1099. Ximena held Valencia until 1102 when she left and burned the city and took El Cid's body with her. Legend has been kind to him.

"In 1492 Burgos lost its place as capital of Castilla to Valladolid but remained an important center.

"In 1812 Burgos was a French stronghold under Napoleon which resisted siege by the Duke of Wellington, and it was 'blown up' by José Bonaparte in 1813.

"Later, the 'Movimiento Nacional' set up a provisional government here in 1936 against the Republicans, and it was here that Francisco Franco was declared 'head of state.'

We arrived in the old city, far more impressive than I had imagined: the medieval walls surrounding it and the huge, fortified gates to the city. Our visit will be short, and we'll do the Cathedral, just for one reason which you'll see soon.

THE CATHEDRAL OF BURGOS

It is the 3rd largest in Spain after Sevilla and Toledo. "Ho hum," someone said, not me. It was begun in 1221 with French, German, and Spanish architects along with those from Flanders in Belgium. It combines flamboyant Gothic and Spanish "Mudéjar."

Tomb of the "Condestables," Burgos

The "Capilla de los Condestables" was done in 1482 with Carrara marble tombs. i.e. El Cid and Doña Ximena. The place seemed very cold, and in fact it was, after all we are on a high plateau in northern Spain. I neglected to mention that before the Cid went into exile, he was in effect a major protector of Alfonso VI as 'Condestable de Castilla,' a medieval county sheriff and enforcer. We all were escorted by a creaky and creepy sacristan inside the usual iron 'reja' steel mesh screen into the center of the nave where one sees on the marble floor no less than the markers for the tombs of El Cid and Doña Ximena. This is the stuff of life and legend and I was moved by the experience. Moved, but not fast enough.

I was trying to get a photo of the tomb when we heard the coach horn honking outside. Uh oh, our driver was indeed ready to depart, a long drive ahead. We turned around to leave, and lo and behold, the large "reja" gate was not only closed but locked. Antônio Saraiva looked over at me, smiled and laughed, and said, "Good thing this didn't happen in León!" After much banging on the gates and shouting, the old sacristan (sorry, he could have done a good imitation of Quasimodo) appeared with a huge key ring, took his time, trying three or four keys (query: had this ever happened before?), and finally opened the creaky gate. We all rushed out, maybe some of us making the sign of the cross and hurried to the coach. Five minutes and we were moving.

"Oh, one perhaps not minor detail: in the small museum inside the church away from the nave there was a glass enclosed, brilliantly lit small Da Vinci. I don't know the title, but it wasn't the Mona Lisa. Sophia somehow missed that museum and was very miffed. We said, "Well, she had blond hair and a nice complexion." "Yeah, Leonardo liked blonds, but … maybe not who you think." Laughter. One of the Spain aficionados on the trip added, "Hey, Queen Sophia is a blond." She retorted, "Yes, but Juan Carlos had to find a chick from Greece and Denmark to get that. He should have gone to Florence. It's complicated."

ON TO ASPEITIA AND LOYOLA CASTLE

It took just two hours with driving through Vitória and an unnamed huge castle off in the distance. The visit to Loyola would be short so we could drive on down to Pamplona and check out that mess.

Bronze of Ignacio Loyola, the Fallen Soldier

I was truly excited to be in the small town where Ignacio de Loyola was born in 1471, grew up as a very late medieval knight battling and evening scores with rivals of his family. And womanizing. (A bit of a "rake"

I would say, but that would change). I won't tell the entire story, but here are the basics: his leg was crushed by a spent cannonball in a battle in 1521 while soldiering for the Duke of Navarra, and he was forced into a long recuperation. Surgeries followed (you can imagine medicine in 1521) with little success and left him with a limp the rest of his life. With nothing to read during the recuperation, someone gave him the "Life of Jesus" and "Lives of the Saints" and they lead to his "conversion."

He wanted to follow the ideal of Francis of Assisi, but was in a sense waylaid when on his planned journey to the Holy Land he did a confession and decision to dedicate his life to Christ at the Benedictine Monastery of Santa María del Monte Serrat. He then lived for about a year in Manresa leading the life of a hermit, spending entire days of prayer in a nearby cave. The idea of reflecting on the life of Christ and putting oneself in the places of the scriptural accounts led to his "Spiritual Exercises." He finally made the trip to the Holy Land in 1523, was recalled by the Benedictines and spent time working in local hospitals. He entered the University of Alcalá de Henares (the same coincidentally as Cervantes) and spent ten years studying theology and Latin. With that preparation he went to Paris in 1535 where he eventually joined with six colleagues and founded the Society of Jesus in 1539, approved by the Pope in 1540. The rest is history – the Society of Jesus and the Jesuits. Famous colleagues like Francisco Xavier and Simão Rodrigues (of Portugal and later fame in India) followed.

That brings me to an interesting turn of events. We all were attending mass in the gorgeous Basilica, I, Father David in clerical blacks, and Sophia in the same pew. I could tell David was deeply moved by it all, and he shortly excused himself saying something about confession. Sophia and I left, went through the Castle – Museum and then had a coffee before heading to the coach.

We know little other than the short explanation later in the coach on the way to Pamplona. David said he asked the celebrant if he could confess, he himself a Jesuit from Goa. The celebrant beamed with happiness to meet a fellow Jesuit, and from Goa!

"Father David, I will be in Goa one month from now to visit your colleagues, and hopefully you. I sincerely hope we can see each other then."

David hemmed and hawed, but managed to stutter, "Of course, that would be wonderful."

What David then revealed was that the mass celebrant was no less than Father Pedro Arrupe, Superior General of the entire Jesuit Order, in Aspeitia on his own pilgrimage and doing a spiritual retreat! I had heard the name but knew little more. It turns out Father Arrupe is also Basque and has led the order in the Post Vatican II era especially in its motto of the "preference for the poor" and Liberation Theology. Some go so far as to call him the "Second Loyola." David would explain later that it was this theology that guided him in his priestly life and teaching in Goa.

"Mike and Amy, this can be nothing less than a spiritual sign for me to continue my life and work at home!

What I did not know and only discovered later from a very distraught Sophia was an episode which took place in Toledo. David had visited Sophia's room and the two had an intimate encounter. I don't know how they resolved the matter, but I do know there was some type of confrontation during the coming night in Zaragoza. A much calmer Sophia would tell me later,

"Miguel, I know you and trust you. I just want you to know that Father David entered my life on this trip and maybe facilitated a life – changing experience. Not only did he console me but through the sacraments gave me a new start in life with a clean slate. And, I think in a way I helped him too. I may never see him again, but I will never forget him."

In an aside to me later on the coach to Barcelona David just said, "Sophia allowed me to no longer have doubts about my virility or manhood. We priests need this; it will sustain me in the future. And also to do my priestly duties. Thank you Mike and AT and IA; I shall return to Goa a better person and priest."

I apologize for spending so much time on this matter, but we cater to our adventurers, and they become part of our story and our lives.

22
ADVENTURES IN ZARAGOZA

The other adventurers who left Salamanca earlier with Harry Downing saw this amazing place before moving on to Barcelona and departure. Most of that group would depart for home. IA would continue its normal route, back through the Mediterranean, down the west coast of Africa, around the cape of Good Hope and on to India. And eventually back to South America and Brazil before once again returning "home" to Portugal. I was sorry I would not be able to make goodbyes to Captain Tony, Exec Martim and others, but had hopes of being reunited with them at some future time. Let's hope so.

Basilica de Nuestra Señora del Pilar, Zaragoza

I surmise most of us were tired, and tired of churches, but this was the "Catholic" or at least more religious part of the expedition adventurers, and

Zaragoza would put the frosting on the cake for all we had seen not just in Spain but in Portugal. The role of the Virgin Mary throughout the history of both countries and of St. James the apostle really began here, and for us, will end here. I'll repeat a little of the story.

St. James, according to legend and belief by much of the western Christian world, had gone to Spain in the hopes of Christianizing those people. He was not having much success, but then, according to legend, there was an apparition of the Virgin to him on the Rio Ebro in 40 A.D. She gave him a column of jasper and an image and asked him to build a church for her in Zaragoza. He did build a chapel. The legend continues: James returned to Jerusalem and was martyred by Herod in 44 A.D. becoming the first Christian martyr. This was the only apparition of Mary before her assumption into heaven.

The original chapel by St. James is long gone, but several churches built upon it followed. And miracles, thus the Basilica of today. They tell you three bombs were dropped on the church in Spain's civil war; none exploded. The legendary pilar of jasper and the image of the Virgin is now on a marble pedestal in one of the chapels. What can I say? The building rivals in my mind the edifices of Sevilla, Toledo, León and Burgos, no small thing. I guess it's different but the same. It was huge, full of stained-glass windows, but in this case the vaults and naves were painted by no less than Goya of 18th century fame, his works already seen in the Prado.

And also tying up loose ends. The Aljafería. It is a a major fortified medieval palace built during the era of the Moorish Taifas (those smaller kingdoms succeeded the Córdoba Caliphate after its fall). Along with Córdoba and Granada, the Aljafería is one of three remaining principal Moslem sites in all Spain. It was the source of Zaragoza Mudéjar style, built outside the old Roman walls (Zaragoza: César Agusto) during the second half of 11th century. It was severely damaged in the Peninsular war (Napoleon) but reconstructed and restored, and as mentioned, survived the bombs of 1936-1939. Some say now that's a miracle we can believe in!

I've jumped ahead, I know, but the Romans were there first, then the Moors and then the Christians with the Reconquest. Amen.

There are several wonderful Paradores in Aragón and nearby Huesca, but Amy arranged for us to stay in a wonderful, beautiful but modern hotel five minutes' walk from the Basilica. There was a huge "Corte Inglés" Spain's most modern department store just two blocks away and was a great chance to finalize shopping for souvenirs. That night at dinner there was more conversation, some now heated, debating the "best" we had seen in Spain – castles, churches, Roman ruins, and yes wine, food and Paradores. All were grateful for Aspeitia and Ignacio de Loyola's castle, and now Zaragoza. I was allowed to repeat (what number of times is this?): "Voy a Zaragoza a comer cigalas en las Plaza de Zaragoza." You might remember the language joke. Maybe it was the occasion, the place or the wine but more people "got" the joke.

23

BARCELONA AND THE DISTURBANCE

The next a.m. was to be the final leg of our "gira" ("Thank God," said Amy.) On to Barcelona and departure for home. Amy would have R and R back home and I would return to Lincoln to get ready for Fall Term. But there's more to tell.

The plan was for the coach to roll into Barcelona late a.m., see Gaudi's "Sagrada Familia," have a final dinner and then all depart for home in England, the U.S., wherever. The ride was a little over three hours and I gave just a short intro to Barcelona – "capital" of Catalonia, its centuries long different history from Castile and central Spain, famous for Las Ramblas commerce and tourist area and most for the "outrageous" (Antônio Saraiva and Maurício Salazar) "unfinished" cathedral. The truth, now almost everyone was mentally and emotionally drained, just a few Gaudi fans among them. "The most hideous building in the world," attributed to George Orwell. Unique it is. I'll say no more.

Adventurers might surmise my opinion. It goes back to some prejudice on the part of my Spanish Ph.D. advisor and passed on to me: "Barcelona, de ninguna manera!" ["Barcelona, no way!"]. The Georgetown Spanish Department had been conducting summer schools in Spain for years, in Sevilla, Madrid and Salamanca. "Not once did we take the kids to

Barcelona. First of all, they only speak Spanish if they have to (Franco outlawed Catalán when he was in power), secondly, they have always wanted to be a separate country back to the 15th century (it was Cataluña that conquered Naples and connected it to Spain during that period of expansion, not to last) and still act like it. Georgetown caught a lot of flak, but as I like to say, "Así sea." ["So be it."]

We did see the "Sagrada Familia." It is unique. I cannot really describe it, don't have the words. I think it belongs in a James Bond movie. I don't wish to end all this marvelous trip on a down note, you're thinking Gaudi, but it was what happened an hour after our visit. A repeat of Madrid! Sirens, police cars everywhere, ETA had exploded a bomb at the Barcelona central police complex. Several people killed. We were hustled back to the coach and offered "tapas" and an early dinner (already set up by Amy) in Barceloneta, the old fishing village and now "hip" area, a nice beach and the Mediterranean in front. Most of us took part, really killing time before all – night "red eye" flights home. We were encouraged by the owner himself that we were indeed safe there and could enjoy the best of seafood and local wines. A small room was reserved just for us.

There was much laughter and reminiscing. A 30 day - plus expedition can create many friendships. Some are "pro -forma:" "Come and visit us in … ." But the close friendships I had made were that indeed. The Peixotos wanted Amy and me to visit in Brazil, Antônio Saraiva said he could arrange a lecture at the University of O Porto or even Coimbra for that matter. And although I did not make close friends from Spain, the adventurers with close ties said we did a good job, a fair job in presenting that country. Of course, the next trip came up: where and when? Amy took the lead on that and said announcements would come via the AT Brochures.

I can't end without the goodbyes to Father David and, uh, Sophia. David hoped he would see Amy when IA did its future trip to Goa and around to Macau and Japan. He gave me a warm embrace, thanking me for everything, and I in turn shared how he had helped me renew admiration for all the Jesuits were doing. I wished him good luck with Father Arrupe. He smiled, said the Father General surely would not have time for him. Sophia offered her thanks, said we should do a land trip to Italy, "Now that would be something to look forward to!" She said she is thinking of doing University when she gets home, perhaps something to do with the rich history of Florence and maybe its relation to the Vatican! "Be careful, you don't know what may be under the stones you turn over." Laughter.

That night Amy and I got on TWA and the long successive flights home, to Madrid, New York, Omaha for me and then Denver for Amy. There is always a letdown after these intense trips and we both were very tired. Too soon to think too much of later trips. We did ponder the idea of proposing a new trip like back in 1974 to Mexico, but to complete the Pre – Colombian picture in Guatemala, Copán in Honduras, and maybe Colombia, but tabled the notion. More important was Mike and Amy. She had promised a decision after this trip, I mean, our future. She surprised the hell out of me.

"Mike, what if we do something modern? You and I can become 'companions' and see how that works? I truly still can't see myself holed up in Lincoln as a faculty wife. But there is still a future for us at AT. You are now secured of a job whenever you want; I am always welcome on the IA. Let's think about it. What do you say?"

"Amy, we are both Catholics, that is, of sorts. I thought marriage was in the works. Maybe you have come up with a 'preferential option for the undecided.' Just for right now. I'm exhausted. Let's go home, rest up, get you back on IA, me in the classroom at Lincoln, and see this Fall how it goes. We hugged and kissed, and both fell into an exhausted sleep.

EPILOGUE

Two related matters happened that August. First there were two letters, each addressed to both Amy and me, one from Father David, another from Sophia.

David informed us he has been invited to be an assistant of Father General Arrupe in Rome and is being promoted to monsignor. He will direct language and cultural studies of India at the Gregorian College in Rome in the Faculty of History and Cultural Heritage of the Church.

Sophia wrote that she is now enrolled in graduate studies in the History Faculty of the U. of Florence, studying the relation of Florentine nobility and the Vatican, so there is a need for research at the Vatican Library. (Our thoughts: will their paths cross?)

The second matter was that later that August James Morrison of AT called us and asked for a meeting at the home office in Los Angeles (not my first, but among many for Amy), to "talk about the future." We met at Los Angeles International, a bit emotional, with hugs and kisses and both saying, "I missed you." We would have the meeting that p.m. and then get reacquainted at the Marriott. James the AT director welcomed us along with Susan Gillian and took us to the conference room. He said he had a call from Harry Downing the Adventure Leader for the International Adventurer on the Peninsula trip. "In sum, and I'm paraphrasing, Harry said 'It was the most contentious trip I've been on for AT, but in some ways the most fun. Amy did yeoman work on the logistics which turned out to be far more complicated with surprises – I mean the ETA bombing in Madrid and again in Barcelona – thus changes in schedules, accommodations, restaurants and most importantly travel home." "And he raved, wrong word, praised you Mike to the high heavens for your work and once more hinted at his retirement. He does that every year, I think I can convince him ($$) to stay awhile.

"The question is, Mike and Amy, you are a team, and do you want to 'carry on' as Harry would say? From our end there's only one answer, 'yes,' but it's your decision."

I said, "James, it was an altogether successful expedition. As long as I can do this in off − time from the U. of N., yes, I'm ready and willing. Amy and I did talk of something of a reprise − not any past trip − but research in Guatemala, a jaunt to Copán, to complete the Pre − Columbian theme. Amy?"

"As long as Xolotl and his crowd are not around! Yes."

James said, "Okay, I think it was part of the original Mexico proposal, I'll pull that out of the files, look it over, and we'll talk later this Fall. So, if you are all right with that, we'll proceed."

We agreed and were off on our own that evening and night with Amy's idea for dinner and then back to the room for more important things, and I don't necessarily mean bedroom time. Dinner was fun, rehashing Portugal and Spain, but more serious conversation took place back at the hotel. I won't go into details, but the conclusion was what was discussed ever so briefly on the plane home from Spain. In short, Mike and Amy would become 'companions' on AT expeditions for the short term, maybe one or two years. She would still have her freedom on AT throughout the year; I would be lonely in Lincoln. Oh well, there's always Big Red Football. Ha!

ABOUT THE AUTHOR

Mark Curran is a retired professor from Arizona State University where he worked from 1968 to 2011. He taught Spanish and Portuguese and their respective cultures. His research specialty was Brazil and its "popular literature in verse" or the "Literatura de Cordel," and he has published many articles in research reviews and now some sixteen books related to the "Cordel" in Brazil, the United States and Spain. Other books done during retirement are of either an autobiographic nature – "The Farm" or "Coming of Age with the Jesuits" - or reflect classes taught at ASU on Luso-Brazilian Civilization, Latin American Civilization or Spanish Civilization. The latter are in the series "Stories I Told My Students:" books on Brazil, Colombia, Guatemala, Mexico, Portugal and Spain. "Letters from Brazil I, II, and III" is an experiment combining reporting and fiction. "A Professor Takes to the Sea I and II" is a chronicle of a retirement adventure with Lindblad Expeditions - National Geographic Explorer. "Rural Odyssey – Living Can Be Dangerous" is "The Farm" largely made fiction. "A Rural Odyssey II – Abilene – Digging Deeper" is a continuation of "Rural Odyssey." "Around Brazil on the 'International Adventurer' – A Panegryic in Fiction" tells of an expedition in better and happier times in Brazil. "Pre – Columbian Mexico Plans, Pitfalls, and Perils" continues the series of fiction and historical narrative. Now, "Portugal and Spain on the 'International Adventurer'" continues that series.

PUBLISHED BOOKS

A Literatura de Cordel. Brasil. 1973

Jorge Amado e a Literatura de Cordel. Brasil. 1981

A Presença de Rodolfo Coelho Cavalcante na Moderna Literatura de Cordel. Brasil. 1987

La Literatura de Cordel – Antología Bilingüe – Español y Portugués. España. 1990

Cuíca de Santo Amaro Poeta-Repórter da Bahia. Brasil. 1991

História do Brasil em Cordel. Brasil. 1998

Cuíca de Santo Amaro – Controvérsia no Cordel. Brasil. 2000

Brazil's Folk-Popular Poetry – "a Literatura de Cordel" – a Bilingual Anthology in English and Portuguese. USA. 2010

The Farm – Growing Up in Abilene, Kansas, in the 1940s and the 1950s. USA. 2010

Retrato do Brasil em Cordel. Brasil. 2011

Coming of Age with the Jesuits. USA. 2012

Peripécias de um Pesquisador "Gringo" no Brasil nos Anos 1960 ou À Cata de Cordel" USA. 2012

Adventures of a 'Gringo' Researcher in Brazil in the 1960s or In Search of Cordel. USA. 2012

A Trip to Colombia – Highlights of Its Spanish Colonial Heritage. USA. 2013

Travel, Research and Teaching in Guatemala and Mexico – In Quest of the Pre-Columbian Heritage

   Volume I – Guatemala. 2013
   Volume II – Mexico. USA. 2013

A Portrait of Brazil in the Twentieth Century – The Universe of the "Literatura de Cordel." USA. 2013

Fifty Years of Research on Brazil – A Photographic Journey. USA. 2013

Relembrando - A Velha Literatura de Cordel e a Voz dos Poetas. USA. 2014

Aconteceu no Brasil – Crônicas de um Pesquisador Norte Americano no Brasil II, USA. 2015

It Happened in Brazil – Chronicles of a North American Researcher in Brazil II. USA, 2015

Diário de um Pesquisador Norte-Americano no Brasil III. USA, 2016

Diary of a North American Researcher in Brazil III. USA, 2016

Letters from Brazil. A Cultural-Historical Narrative Made Fiction. USA 2017.

A Professor Takes to the Sea – Learning the Ropes on the National Geographic Explorer.

   Volume I, "Epic South America" 2013 USA, 2018.
   Volume II, 2014 and "Atlantic Odyssey 108" 2016, USA, 2018

Letters from Brazil II – Research, Romance and Dark Days Ahead. USA, 2019.

A Rural Odyssey – Living Can Be Dangerous. USA, 2019.

Letters from Brazil III – From Glad Times to Sad Times. USA, 2019.

A Rural Odyssey II – Abilene – Digging Deeper. USA, 2020

Around Brazil on the 'International Adventurer' – A Panegyric in Fiction, USA, 2020

Pre – Columbian Mexico, Plans, Pitfalls and Perils. USA 2020

Portugal and Spain on the "International Adventurer." USA 2020

Professor Curran lives in Mesa, Arizona, and spends part of the year in Colorado. He is married to Keah Runshang Curran and they have one daughter Kathleen who lives in Albuquerque, New Mexico, married to teacher Courtney Hinman in 2018. Her documentary film "Greening the Revolution" was presented most recently in the Sonoma Film Festival in California, this after other festivals in Milan, Italy and New York City. Katie was named best female director in the Oaxaca Film Festival in Mexico.

The author's e-mail address is: profmark@asu.edu
His website address is: www.currancordelconnection.com

Printed in the United States
By Bookmasters